The Masterworks of Literature Series

WILLIAM S. OSBORNE, *Editor*

Southern Connecticut State College

Kavanagh

KAVANAGH

A Tale

by HENRY WADSWORTH LONGFELLOW

Edited for the Modern Reader by
Jean Downey
SOUTHERN CONNECTICUT STATE COLLEGE

COLLEGE & UNIVERSITY PRESS · *Publishers*
NEW HAVEN, CONN.

New Material, Introduction and Notes
by JEAN DOWNEY

MANUFACTURED IN THE UNITED STATES OF AMERICA BY
UNITED PRINTING SERVICES, INC.
NEW HAVEN, CONNECTICUT

Introduction

Village life, from *Plymouth Plantation* to *Peyton Place,* is always of interest. *Kavanagh,* written more than one hundred years ago, is also a village tale that has all the ingredients of a good New England recipe: old maids and young maids, lotharios, clergymen, tradesmen, a schoolteacher, a magazinist, a taxidermist, suicides (one by design; two by default), runaways, travelers, odd characters, good and bad characters. Additionally, Longfellow's own life and time spill over into it giving it genuine flavor, even though to some the entire mixture is mild, especially to "palates spoiled by spices."

Slight in appearance as well as in plot, *Kavanagh* is the last of Longfellow's excursions into long prose fiction, *Outre-Mer* (1835) and *Hyperion* (1839) being the first. In between these dates, of course, Longfellow was at work on short stories, essays, anthologies, and poetry, with one of his best known pieces— "Evangeline"—completed the very day he started *Kavanagh.* As a matter of fact, two entries in his journal disclose, in part, his purpose in writing the tale. "Evangeline is ended. I wrote the last lines this morning. And now for a little prose; a romance, which I have in my brain,—Kavanagh by name."[1] Ostensibly this might be reason enough for writing *Kavanagh*—a change of pace from poetry to prose. Yet another entry, which does not even mention *Kavanagh,* is far more interesting principally for what it does not emphasize: Longfellow's ambition. This item reads: "Lowell passed the evening with us. His Fable for Critics is thought by all to be very witty. His Biglow poems will soon be out, and also a Christmas poem; making three books this autumn."[2] At the time, Lowell was twenty-nine (Longfellow was forty-one) and, according to N. P. Willis, the "best launched

---

[1] Samuel Longfellow, *Life of Henry Wadsworth Longfellow* (Boston, 1886), II, p. 81. Cited hereafter as *Life,* I, II.

[2] *Ibid.,* II, 127-28.

man of his time." And the word was out among the critics that Lowell was the poet of the future.

In toting up Lowell's productions, Longfellow must have looked to his own. Was he keeping pace? Whatever his own answer, Longfellow's journal for the day before Lowell's visit says: "In the evening finished Kavanagh."[3] This achievement, his already successful "Evangeline," and some other verse undoubtedly helped him to remember a statement he had made to his father some years before: "I will be eminent in something."[4] Actually Longfellow always cared, indeed was always very much aware of the amount and kind of literature produced by his contemporaries at home and abroad, and while he was realistic and sensible enough not to try to match their output, he was at the same time sufficiently mindful of the purposes and plans he had announced for himself in his youth:

> The fact is ... I most eagerly aspire after future eminence in literature; my whole soul burns most ardently for it, and every earthly thought centres in it. . . . Surely, there never was a better opportunity offered for the exertion of literary talent in our own country than is now offered. . . . Whether Nature has given me any capacity for knowledge or not, she has at any rate given me a very strong predilection for literary pursuits, and I am almost confident in believing, that, if I ever rise in the world, it must be by the exercise of my talent in the wide field of literature.[5]

Besides all of this, Longfellow was of Puritan stock: he dreaded the waste of time, especially the time left for writing after attending to his professorial duties at Harvard where he had been teaching modern languages since 1836.

No matter its purpose—real or fancied—*Kavanagh* at first just filled a gap. "When evening came I really missed the poem ["Evangeline"] and the pencil. Instead thereof I wrote a chapter of Kavanagh."[6] For the next year or more, Longfellow continued

[3] *Ibid.*
[4] *Ibid.*, I, 56.
[5] *Ibid.*, pp. 53-54.
[6] *Ibid.*, II, 82.

to record his progress and his feelings about *Kavanagh*. Once he said: "wrote in Kavanagh, to my own great satisfaction and delight."[7] Another entry noted: "worked very briskly and breezily"[8] and still another: "Worked at Kavanagh; or played at it . . . it being very pleasant and easy work."[9] When it was nearly completed he commented: "I have written it *con amore*, and have had so much satisfaction as this, whatsoever may be its fate hereafter."[10] But the writing of *Kavanagh* was not all cakes and ale. From its inception on February 27, 1847, to its release on May 12, 1849, it met with delays, some attributable to ennui, others to lack of time. For example, the day after Longfellow started *Kavanagh* he had to put it aside, for a new semester had commenced at Harvard and in addition to lecturing, he attended lectures, answered correspondence, interviewed writers, would-be-writers, editors, and publishers, wrote poetry, read, entertained at Craigie House (his home in Cambridge), and loved his wife and children. Even summer vacations helped in the postponement: "I find it quite impossible to write in the country. The influences are soothing and slumberous. In coming here [the Melville house, not far from the home of Dr. Holmes, in Pittsfield, Massachusetts] I hoped to work successfully on Kavanagh; and as yet I have written scarcely a page . . ."[11]

Actually, the bulk of *Kavanagh* was not written until the fall of 1848 and supposedly finished that November. But even then it was not quite right and as late as January 21, 1849, Longfellow said: "Read [the manuscript] of Kavanagh to Sumner, F., and S. The general opinion favorable, on the whole, though it did not awaken any very lively enthusiasm."[12] Approximately a month later his journal reveals his hesitancy, even his annoyance:

[7] *Ibid.*, p. 124.
[8] *Ibid.*, p. 125.
[9] *Ibid.*, p. 126.
[10] *Ibid.*, p. 127.
[11] *Ibid.*, p. 120.
[12] *Ibid.*, p. 131.

With some doubts and misgivings, I carried the first sheets of Kavanagh to the printer. I have never hesitated so much about any of my books, except the first hexameters, "The Children of the Lord's Supper." Let us see how it will look in print. I want to get this out of the way. Things lying in manuscript incumber and impede me; hold me back from working on to something better. . . .[13]

One month more was to go by before he was struck with the thought that another chapter must go into the book "as the key-stone into the arch. An idea so very obvious, and yet coming so late."[14] Finally on May 12, 1849, *Kavanagh* was published, notwithstanding Longfellow's perplexity about the title.

Book titles are usually interesting; sometimes they are even provocative. Such has been the case with *Kavanagh* since its very beginning. Just before the book was scheduled to appear in 1849, its publishers, Ticknor, Reed, and Fields, a reputable as well as an influential firm, managed to have planted in the right publications advance notices of Longfellow's newest work. This item, for instance, appeared in the Boston *Evening Transcript:*

> We notice in several of the papers a reference to Mr. Longfellow's new book (which Ticknor & Co. promise in May,) to the effect that it is a *poem,* and that the subject of it is a story of *Ireland.* We can correct this statement from an authentic source. Kavanagh is a prose story, written somewhat in the style of Hyperion, and the incidents occur in a New England village of the present day. That it will be a beautiful picture of life in our own times, no one who has read Mr. Longfellow's prose works will hesitate to believe. It will no doubt be the book of the spring, and will probably meet with a success, judging from present indications almost unprecedented in the American book market.[15]

Longfellow's wife, Fanny Appleton Longfellow, was not much struck with the name, but to Longfellow himself it was "sonorous."[16] Later, however, he was not so certain. "The title is

[13] *Ibid.,* p. 134.
[14] *Ibid.,* p. 136.
[15] *Daily Evening Transcript* (Boston), April 3, 1849, p. 2.
[16] *Life,* II, 125.

better than the book, and suggests a different kind of book. . . ."[17] he records in his journal. With this Emerson would agree: "I was deceived by the fine name into a belief that there was some family legend. . . ."[18] Just what there was about the name Kavanagh and a family legend is a bit obscure and surely not important now but there must have been something to it at the time, for just prior to the publication of the book Longfellow made this entry in his journal: "We passed the evening at the Nortons' to meet the G——'s of Maine, who tell me that the Kavanagh family has quite died out there, and the little church has been closed."[19] For all that, however, *Kavanagh* is still a fascinating title. To the initiate it is a ready reference to a discussion of universalism versus nationalism in literature (Chapter XX), to the American literature buff it is an opportunity to prove that Longfellow wrote prose as well as poetry, and to the new reader, mindful of esthetic distance, it is a charming tale of the way our people used to live.

The way it was with those people is told entirely by an omniscient author who steps aside only briefly on two occasions to let a schoolgirl with just the right touch account for some of the village doings. The main events all occur within a year's time and the happenings in Fairmeadow during the three years' absence of two of the principal characters are capsuled in two final chapters.

Kavanagh is not really all about Arthur Kavanagh; at least it is not all his story. It is Mr. Churchill's story. But he lets it go by default; he permits Kavanagh to walk off with the action, while he dreams and dawdles away the days. To be a writer is Mr. Churchill's hope; to be a schoolmaster is his lot, and all the material for romance which can come to him quite handily is lost simply because he could not see it: "the nearer incidents of aspiration, love, and death, escaped him."[20]

Some of the other characters around which the tale revolves

[17] *Ibid.,* p. 135.
[18] *Ibid.,* p. 140.
[19] *Ibid.,* p. 136.
[20] Henry Wadsworth Longfellow, *Kavanagh, A Tale* (Boston, 1849), p. 114.

are drawn airily. Alice Archer, pretty but poor and pale, rises out of the canvas appealingly to stand beside Cecilia Vaughan, her schoolmate and dearest friend, who is beautiful, rich, and vital. Both girls are in love with the young, energetic Kavanagh who is a successor to Mr. Pendexter, the village parson dismissed by his congregation after twenty-five years of service.

By turn the story is sentimental and humorous with, as in many tales of the time, persons in the lower class providing the humor. Sally Manchester, an excellent maid and a very bad cook, is engaged to an itinerant dentist "who, in filling her teeth with amalgam, had seized the opportunity to fill a soft place in her heart with something still more dangerous and mercurial."[21] The letter of dentist Martin Cherryfield to Sally Manchester, telling her that he was going to marry someone else is a forerunner of that written by Chas. F. Lewis to Mabelle Gillespie in Ring Lardner's "Some Like Them Cold." H. Adolphus Hawkins, a linen draper whose "shiny hair went off to the left in a superb sweep, like the handrail of a bannister,"[22] was the village beau as well as a poet; in fact, he was so much a poet that as his sister frequently remarked, "he spoke blank verse in the bosom of his family."[23] Silas, another swain, wrote love letters in his own blood. He waded barefoot in the brook to be bitten by leeches and then used his feet as inkstands. Mr. Wilmerdings, the butcher, also had many interesting sides: five pensionary cats who stood by his cart daily for their meal, a scale used to weigh provisions as well as babies, and the memory of a bridal tour when he and Mrs. Wilmerdings went to a neighboring town to see a man hanged for murdering his wife.

As a story *Kavanagh* is not remarkable and its incidents are few. One concerns the orphaned fifteen-year-old Lucy, the Churchill's maid, who wandered from the village with a bootmaker. When she returned, "forlorn and forsaken," she was

[21] *Ibid.*, p. 45.
[22] *Ibid.*, p. 66.
[23] *Ibid.*, p. 67.

often heard to say she wished she were only a Christian that she might destroy her life. Under the exciting influences of a Millerite camp meeting one evening she drowned herself in the river. Much of the moment is therefore in *Kavanagh* from the mention of "that fanatical sect [the Millerites] who believed the end of the world was imminent, and had prepared their ascension robes to be lifted up in clouds of glory,"[24] to the life and scenery of Maine and the Berkshire Hills, to Longfellow's own domestic relations. Of course, in Churchill there are indications of Longfellow's early conflicts, his duties battling with his desires. Longfellow wanted to devote all of his time to writing yet he was to wait five more years, until 1854, to resign his professorship at Harvard. Meanwhile, the poetizing ladies of Fairmeadow considered Churchill the true light of literature for that part of the world and they inflicted their dainty manuscripts upon him without qualm. Clarissa Cartwright not only wanted Mr. Churchill's candid opinion of her "Symphonies of the Soul, and Other Poems" but should also be delighted to have him "write a Preface, to introduce the work to the public. The publisher says it would increase the sale very considerably."[25] Another visitor, Mr. Hathaway, the projector of a new magazine that was "to raise the character of American literature" played upon the right strings and had Churchill's promise to write for this forthcoming publication—which never came into being—a series of papers on "Obscure Martyrs," "a kind of tragic history of the unrecorded and life-long sufferings of women, which hitherto had found no historians, save now and then a novelist."[26]

Unfortunately, posterity proved that Longfellow was not a novelist and *Kavanagh* not a tale. Some reviewers of the time thought so too, but they were not many, most of Longfellow's contemporaries having a high regard for his newest fiction. Emerson said in a letter: "I think it the best sketch we have

[24] *Ibid.,* p. 96.
[25] *Ibid.,* p. 101.
[26] *Ibid.,* p. 90.

seen in the direction of the American novel. For here is our native speech and manners, treated with sympathy, taste, and judgment."[27] From the Custom House on June 5, 1849, Nathaniel Hawthorne wrote:

> Dear Longfellow,—I meant to have written you before now about Kavanagh, but have had no quiet time during my letter-writing hours, and now the freshness of my thoughts has exhaled away. It is a most precious and rare book; as fragant as a bunch of flowers, and as simple as one flower. A true picture of life, moreover,—as true as those reflections of the trees and banks that I used to see in the Concord; but refined to a higher degree than they, as if the reflection itself were reflected. Nobody but yourself would dare to write so quiet a book; nor could any other succeed in it. It is entirely original, a book by itself; a true work of genius if ever there were one. And yet I should not wonder if many people (confound them!) were to see no such matter in it. In fact, I doubt whether anybody else has enjoyed it so much as I, although I have heard or seen none but favorable opinions. I should like to have written a long notice of it, and would have done so for the Salem Advertiser; but on the strength of my notice of Evangeline and some half-dozen other books, I have been accused of a connection with the editorship of that paper, and of writing political articles,—which I never did one single time in my life! . . . Ever your friend, Nath. Hawthorne.[28]

Of special interest to some contemporary reviewers of *Kavanagh* were its length, imitativeness, and its classification as a tale. To Bayard Taylor of the New York *Tribune* the brevity of the book was one of its greatest charms: "The story of Kavanagh is told in very few words; in incident, description and reflection it is compressed and very brief, though everywhere suggestive of all that is not told. Every tempting opportunity to digress from the simple, unadorned narrative has been scrupulously resisted."[29] To *Graham's Magazine* the contrary was true:

> There is one fault to the book more serious, perhaps, than any other, and that is its shortness. The characters are well con-

---

[27] *Life*, II, 140.
[28] *Ibid.*, pp. 141-42.
[29] New York *Daily Tribune*, May 10, 1849, p. 1.

ceived, but imperfectly developed. The premises of Kavanagh's character are excellent, but no conclusion is drawn from them except his marriage, and that is something of a non-sequitur. The ground is fairly broken for a long work, for a sort of American Wilhelm Meister, and though the author's plan hardly demands its cultivation to the extent of its capacity, we feel rather provoked that he did not make his plan commensurate with the elements of his characters.[30]

On this point Longfellow himself said, "People think it not long enough. But why beat out one's ideas into thin leaf?"[31] *Brownson's Quarterly Review* was not only in agreement with him but also delighted

> to discover that the author meant to tell his tale by a few brief masterly touches, instead of inflating pages with useless expiation, explanation, and analysis, conformably to the prevailing vicious fashion. As books multiply they ought to be brief. . . . If we must have fiction, let it consist of meaningful outlines, that in a glance we may enjoy it. . . . What is the condition of English and French fiction at this moment? Volume after volume, fine print, rolled off with incredible velocity,—vast masses of love, lust, and battle, heaped up high as a pyramid. Everything for quantity, nothing for quality. . . .[32]

Many of the reviewers saw much of Dickens and the German Romantic, Jean Paul Richter, in Longfellow's narration, and while the man from *Brownson's* admitted the imitation of Dickens to be successful, especially that of Hawkins and Sally Manchester, he was made unhappy by some other influences, for "Mr. Churchill's dream smacks too strongly of Hans Christian Andersen, and in many passages there is a vein of Goethe."[33] According to the *Southern Quarterly Review*, however, it was just this borrowing from the German that gave *Kavanagh* some of its quaintness. Whereas the *American Review* merely mentioned Lamartine, *Godey's Lady's Book* went some steps beyond:

[30] *Graham's American Monthly Magazine*, XXXV (July, 1849), 71.
[31] *Life*, II, 140.
[32] *Brownson's Quarterly Review*, IV (January, 1850), 77.
[33] *Ibid.*, p. 85.

We hardly know a work of fiction we would so cordially commend to the youth of both sexes. What a contrast between "Kavanagh" and Lamartine's late novel "Raphael"! These two works are most significant proofs of the moral difference in the character of the people of France and America.[34]

Whether or not *Kavanagh* was a tale concerned some reviewers. One said it "is a sketch and not properly a rounded and complete story."[35] Another called it a novelette, two thought of it as a sort of prose pastoral, and with this a third would agree, while at the same time offering a suggestion or two, as well as a complaint:

> The word "Tale," upon the title page, if it be not merely a formal suffix, like the "Esq." in the address of all American letters, we consider a misnomer. We think a truer name for the book would be, a prose pastoral. It had been better to have called it "Kavanagh" simply, and left it to the reader to find out what it was. And it is not as a reader, but as a critic, that we make the complaint.[36]

A major consideration of many critics was Longfellow's handling of characters, especially the two "heroines" Alice Archer and Cecilia Vaughan. *The Literary World* considered the two, "ideals of pathos and happiness."[37] But no such girls could be found, especially in New England, said *The American Review:*

> In no such village could Miss Vaughan, there born and bred, have preserved that aristocratic exclusiveness which limited her acquaintance to Alice Archer, and held her at such awful, unapproachable distance above the unfortunate aspirations of Mr. Adolphus Hawkins. Alice Archer is more true to nature. [But] . . . The practical morality squeezed from her story, and thrown, as it were, in the teeth of poor, innocent, Mr. Churchill, is so wide as to be ridiculous, and makes one laugh as if at the wrong time. . . .[38]

[34] *Godey's Lady's Book*, XXXIX (July, 1849), 79.
[35] *Christian Examiner*, XLVII (July, 1849), 154.
[36] *North American Review*, LXIX (July, 1849), 213. James Russell Lowell reviewed *Kavanagh* in this issue.
[37] *Literary World*, IV (May 26, 1849), 452.
[38] *American Review*, X (July, 1849), 62.

Brownson's Quarterly Review showed a partiality for the delineation of Alice Archer.

> Alice is more distinct, and better drawn than her friend, for this very obvious reason,—that it is infinitely easier to portray the real feeling of a melancholy child of nature, than catch and convey the true character of a woman with a light heart and something of the world in her.[39]

Quite swept away by the friendship of the two girls, a young man at Yale said:

> The attachment and intimacy of these two young girls is one of the most charming pictures in the book. It is a constant and beautiful rehearsal of the "great drama of woman's life." It seems too pure, too artless, too confiding, for such a world as this.[40]

A present-day view of the two friends is in Arvin's book on Longfellow:

> the fair, delicate, oversensitive Alice Archer and the ardent Cecilia Vaughan, . . . are, according to Longfellow, "in love with each other." Their relations might have formed a study in what James spoke of as "those friendships between women which are so common in New England," and which he dramatized so veraciously in *The Bostonians*. But there is so little human reality in either Alice or Cecilia—they are observed at such a gingerly distance and characterized so diaphanously—that they cannot be compared for a moment with Olive Chancellor and Verena Tarrant.[41]

In truth, Longfellow pleased and displeased with his characters. While one reviewer was saying that the characters were not developed, another believed them to be "sketched with such fidelity to nature that the reader thinks them real persons who really lived in some actual Fairmeadow."[42] None, however, missed the transparent moral, "The Flighty purpose never is o'ertook,/Unless the deed go with it." And the choice of the

---

[39] *Brownson's*, p. 78.
[40] *Yale Literary Magazine*, XIV (August, 1849), 388.
[41] Newton Arvin, *Longfellow: His Life and Work* (Boston, 1963), p. 129.
[42] *Massachusetts Quarterly Review*, II (June, 1849), 387.

motto indicates what the context confirms: that Churchill is the real hero of the book, whatever Kavanagh may be allegorically. Yet both men were the heroes according to *The American Review*:

> Though Kavanagh is the ostensible hero, Churchill, the village schoolmaster, is really the predominant character. We might not improperly consider them as twin heroes—not in the ancient signification truly, but by the complaisance of novel technicality. They possess little individuality, and reversed circumstances might have fitted either to sit for the portrait of the other. They are both sentimental, both pedantic; and we never lose sight of them. Like Castor and Pollux, when one is not endeavoring to shine, the other is always sure to display *his* light.[43]

Mr. Pendexter, one of Mr. Churchill's friends, is carefully drawn and has, for at least one reviewer, more original points than many other characters in the tale. Before he left the village of Fairmeadow, Pendexter preached a withering valedictory to his parishioners. And this "quaint bold sermon" was not an imaginary discourse according to *The Christian Examiner*. "We have seen a printed copy of the original, and it deserves to be mentioned, that the clergyman who really preached it, and who supposed it would be his last in the parish to which he ministered, did remain with them several years longer."[44] In his farewell sermon Pendexter told the congregation "that they were so confirmed in their bad habits, that no reformation was to be expected in them under his ministry, and that to produce one would require a greater exercise of Divine power than it did to create the world; for in creating the world there had been no opposition."[45]

In contrast to Pendexter is Kavanagh, a cultivated and sensitive reformer who "did not so much denounce vice, as inculcate virtue; he did not deny, but affirm; he did not lacerate the hearts of his hearers with doubt and disbelief, but consoled,

[43] *Brownson's,* p. 59.
[44] *Christian Examiner,* p. 154.
[45] *Kavanagh,* pp. 43-44.

and comforted, and healed them with faith."[46] Kavanagh's Catholic Maine ancestors, his early years spent on the shores and in the forests of Maine, his Jesuit college education in Canada, and then his conversion to Protestantism make up Chapter XVIII. Incidentally, a week in advance of the book's release, *The Literary World*, edited at the time by the Duyckincks, had reprinted in its columns the entire chapter concerning the early years of Kavanagh. This reprint then was a primary lauding of *Kavanagh;* later, fuller, praise coming in a review which said the book was one "to give pleasure and promote refinement."[47] A few biographers see in *Kavanagh* some of Longfellow's own religious beliefs; in fact Cecil Williams says:

> There are numerous hints at his religious beliefs throughout his poetry, but perhaps his most forthright treatment of religion is in *Kavanagh*. He introduces the Reverend Arthur Kavanagh as a descendant of an ancient Catholic family which had settled in Maine. Arthur had attended a Jesuit college, but his search for truth and freedom had converted him to Protestantism. However, "He had but passed from one chapel to another in the same vast cathedral" . . . bringing from the old faith what was holy and pure but leaving behind it bigotry, fanaticism, and intolerance. Kavanagh does not have the bigotry of his Calvinistic predecessor, Mr. Pendexter. Longfellow describes Kavanagh in his study: "The study in the tower was delightful. There sat the young apostle, and meditated the great design and purpose of his life, the removal of all prejudice, and uncharitableness, and persecution, and the union of all sects into one church universal." . . . Apparently Longfellow regarded Arthur Kavanagh with approval; if so, he was at this time clearly a liberal Unitarian.[48]

Edward Wagenknecht, some years earlier, said substantially the same as Williams regarding Longfellow and Unitarianism as evidenced in *Kavanagh*: "Kavanagh takes his texts from the Gospels, denounces vice less than he praises virtue, practices open communion, and defies sectarianism. In much of this he

[46] *Ibid.,* p. 102.
[47] *Literary World,* p. 451.
[48] Cecil Williams, *Henry Wadsworth Longfellow* (New York, 1964), p. 123.

is in harmony with Channing's teaching, for the great Unitarian maintained 'that he did not belong to any one sect but rather to the community of those free minds who loved the truth.' "[49] Insofar as Longfellow and Catholicism are concerned, Wagenknecht says:

and the account of Arthur Kavanagh's "emancipation" from his inherited Catholic faith generally pleases them [Catholic readers] as little as the universal church he wishes to establish, in which all distinctively Christian doctrines and ordinances are scrapped, and where "active charity" (which has never been absent from Catholicism) takes the place of creeds.[50]

On the other hand, a few persons had somewhat different reactions to Kavanagh's conversion. The reviewer from *Brownson's Quarterly*, for instance, commended Longfellow for his good taste in making "Kavanagh's conversion to Protestantism sentimental instead of logical";[51] and Newton Arvin recently said: "Kavanagh, indeed, is not a realized character, but a mere projection of Longfellow's generous though extremely misty, theological ideas."[52]

Chapters XIII and XX in this tale were to cause much comment. The first of these, Chapter XIII, concerns Mr. Churchill and his "pulpit eloquence."

Mr. Churchill had really put up in his study the old, white, wineglass-shaped pulpit. It served as a playhouse for his children, who, whether in it or out of it, daily preached to his heart, and were a living illustration of the way to enter into the kingdom of heaven. Moreover, he himself made use of it externally as a notebook, recording his many meditations with a pencil on the white panels.[53]

Strong objection was made to this section by the *North American Review*: "the division numbered thirteen has no manner of business in the book. We feel it as an unwarrantable intrusion,

[49] Edward Wagenknecht, *Longfellow: A Full-Length Portrait* (New York, 1955), p. 296.
[50] *Ibid.*, p. 295.
[51] *Brownson's*, p. 82.
[52] Arvin, p. 127.
[53] *Kavanagh*, p. 56.

and do not at once recover our composure."[54] This chapter was also considered an error of judgment by the *American Review*:

Mr. Churchill's use of the old church pulpit is preposterously improbable, since its dimensions may reasonably be supposed to have equalled the capacity of his study to receive it, and greatly to have exceeded the width of an inner door. It is laughable to observe with what forethought and labor it is brought up, and made to serve in presenting with an easy, natural air these meditations, which, after all, we read with little interest, because however beautiful or brilliant in themselves, they stand separate and disconnected. Brought in as illustrations, such things possess a charm which is lost when we see them alone. Forced upon us without propriety they become wearisome.... Another objection might be offered to this "pulpit eloquence" as it is facetiously termed, in that it draws from the story and its personages, and brings the author before us in their stead....[55]

Chapter XX provided the liveliest interest for the literary men of the day because in the 1840's nationality in literature was being discussed quite stormily in America's leading periodicals. This section of the tale, which continues still to be anthologized, is a dialogue between Mr. Churchill and the national-literature man, Mr. Hathaway. When Hathaway says to Churchill: "But you admit nationality to be a good thing?" Churchill replies: "Yes, if not carried too far ... I prefer what is natural. Mere nationality is often ridiculous."[56] Then, when queried on his thoughts of national literature, Churchill said:

"Simply, that a national literature is not the growth of a day. Centuries must contribute their dew and sunshine to it. Our own is growing slowly but surely, striking its roots downward, and its branches upward, as is natural; and I do not wish, for the sake of what some people call originality, to invert it, and try to make it grow with its roots in the air. And as for having it so savage and wild as you want it, I have only to say, that all literature, as well as all art, is the result of culture and intellectual refinement."[57]

[54] *North American Review,* p. 214.
[55] *American Review,* p. 64.
[56] *Kavanagh,* p. 86.
[57] *Ibid.,* p. 87.

In *The Raven and The Whale,* Perry Miller says that Hathaway is a satire on Cornelius Mathews, a New York editor. And "If Mr. Hathaway's rhodomontade is a parody of Cornelius Mathews—and even, by anticipation, of Whitman—" says Newton Arvin, "Mr. Churchill's rejoinders are an unintentional parody of the universalists, so tepid are they, so stale in thought, so peppered with exasperating half-truths." It is also Arvin's opinion that "In making the schoolmaster a mouthpiece for such views, Longfellow made him, for the moment, a complacent bore."[58]

Much more than literary quarrels interested the general reading public in 1849, however; for example, among the new American books were Melville's *Mardi,* Parkman's *The Oregon Trail,* Whittier's *Margaret Smith's Journal,* Thoreau's *Week on the Concord and Merrimack,* Southworth's *Retribution,* and Griswold's *Female Poets of America.* The regulars of course included Washington Irving, who was superintending the new issue of his complete works, and Cooper, who would soon be in the field with a uniform edition of his books. Here it is interesting to note that the reviewer for the *Southern Quarterly* considered Cooper a better writer than Longfellow, in at least one respect: Cooper did not force comparisons; Longfellow did. At the time the reviewer said: "We turn to a book [*The Sea-Lions,* just published] of Mr. Cooper, a writer of very different order, and who takes no pains in the search after metaphor and illustration. . . ."[59] As an example of Longfellow's extravagance of comparison the reviewer offered this: "The ringing of a Sabbath bell is likened to the explosion of a brazen mortar (which the bell really is)—'bombarding the village with bursting shells of sound.' The striking of the clock reminds him 'of Jael driving the nail into the head of Sisera, &c.' "[60] It is only fair to add, however, that the reviewer considered these failures amusing and that he believed Longfellow to be "a careful writer."

Undoubtedly the thrilling adventures and the wild Indianism

[58] Arvin, p. 128.
[59] *Southern Quarterly Review,* XXXI (October, 1849), 246.
[60] *Ibid.*

that came from the pen of Cooper were much more to the liking of the American people than the picturesque homeliness which Longfellow believed to be the general sentiment. Nevertheless, Longfellow occupied more space in the popular imagination of his day than any other author; and *Kavanagh* does have its special value, though assuredly not for the literary clinician, for here is no Longfellow "wound" and no place to hunt down symbols. *Kavanagh* is simply a delightful, charming account of a small world within itself; a tale of the way life used to be. It is a souvenir of the past.

JEAN DOWNEY

Southern Connecticut State College

SELECTED BIBLIOGRAPHY

Books

Arvin, Newton, *Longfellow: His Life and Work.* Boston: Little, Brown, 1963.

Longfellow, Henry Wadsworth. *Kavanagh, A Tale.* Boston: Ticknor, Reed, and Fields, 1849.

Longfellow, Samuel. *Life of Henry Wadsworth Longfellow.* Boston: Ticknor and Company, 1886, 2 vols.

Miller, Perry. *The Raven and the Whale.* New York: Harcourt, Brace & World, 1956.

Wagenknecht, Edward. *Longfellow: A Full-Length Portrait.* New York: Longmans, Green, 1955.

Williams, Cecil. *Henry Wadsworth Longfellow.* New York: Twayne, 1964.

Periodicals

American Review, X (July, 1849), 57-66.

Brownson's Quarterly Review, IV (January, 1850), 56-87.

Christian Examiner, XLVII (July, 1849), 153-54.

Eclectic Magazine, XVII (August, 1849), 575-76.

Godey's Lady's Book, XXXIX (July, 1849), 79.

Graham's American Monthly Magazine, XXXV (July, 1849), 71.

Holden's Dollar Magazine, IV (July, 1849), 436-38; (August, 1849), 506-7.

Knickerbocker, XXXIII (June, 1849), 538-40.

Literary World, IV (May 5, 1849), 389-90; (May 26, 1849), 451-52.

Massachusetts Quarterly Review, II (June, 1849), 386-87.

North American Review, LXIX (July, 1849), 196-215; CIV (April, 1867), 531-40.

Sartain's Union Magazine of Literature and Art, V (July, 1849), 64.

Southern Literary Messenger, XV (July, 1849), 436-37.

Southern Quarterly Review, XVI (October, 1849), 245-46.

Yale Literary Magazine, XIV (August, 1849), 381-91; XL (February, 1875), 261-65.

Newspapers

Daily Evening Transcript (Boston), April 3, 1849, p. 2.
New York *Daily Tribune,* May 10, 1849, p. 1.

Contents

A NOTE ON THE TEXT

This edition reproduces the text of the first edition, published in 1849 by Ticknor, Reed, and Fields. There were at least four issues printed that year, designated in order of issue as A, B, C, and D. The text of this edition has been set from the most common issue, C, except for some changes in hyphenation, spelling, and capitalization.

I

GREAT men stand like solitary towers in the city of God, and secret passages running deep beneath external nature give their thoughts intercourse with higher intelligences, which strengthens and consoles them, and of which the laborers on the surface do not even dream!

Some such thought as this was floating vaguely through the brain of Mr. Churchill, as he closed his schoolhouse door behind him; and if in any degree he applied it to himself, it may perhaps be pardoned in a dreamy, poetic man like him; for we judge ourselves by what we feel capable of doing, while others judge us by what we have already done. And moreover his wife considered him equal to great things. To the people in the village, he was the schoolmaster, and nothing more. They beheld in his form and countenance no outward sign of the divinity within. They saw him daily moiling and delving in the common path, like a beetle, and little thought that underneath that hard and cold exterior, lay folded delicate golden wings, wherewith, when the heat of day was over, he soared and reveled in the pleasant evening air.

Today he was soaring and reveling before the sun had set; for it was Saturday. With a feeling of infinite relief he left behind him the empty schoolhouse, into which the hot sun of a September afternoon was pouring. All the bright young faces were gone; all the impatient little hearts were gone; all the fresh voices, shrill, but musical with the melody of childhood, were gone; and the lately busy realm was given up to silence, and the dusty sunshine, and the old gray flies, that buzzed and bumped their heads against the window panes. The sound of the outer door, creaking on its hebdomadal hinges, was like a sentinel's challenge, to which the key growled responsive in the lock; and the master, casting a furtive glance at the last caricature of himself in red chalk on the wooden fence close by, entered with a light step the solemn avenue of pines that led to the margin of the river.

At first his step was quick and nervous; and he swung his cane as if aiming blows at some invisible and retreating enemy. Though a meek man, there were moments when he remembered with bitterness the unjust reproaches of fathers and their insulting words; and then he fought imaginary battles with people out of sight, and struck them to the ground, and trampled upon them; for Mr. Churchill was not exempt from the weakness of human nature, nor the customary vexations of a schoolmaster's life. Unruly sons and unreasonable fathers did sometimes embitter his else sweet days and nights. But as he walked, his step grew slower, and his heart calmer. The coolness and shadows of the great trees comforted and satisfied him, and he heard the voice of the wind as it were the voice of spirits calling around him in the air. So that when he emerged from the black woodlands into the meadows by the river's side, all his cares were forgotten.

He lay down for a moment under a sycamore, and thought of the Roman Consul Licinius, passing a night with eighteen of his followers in the hollow trunk of the great Lycian plane-tree. From the branches overhead the falling seeds were wafted away through the soft air on plumy tufts of down. The continuous murmur of the leaves and of the swift-running stream seemed rather to deepen than disturb the pleasing solitude and silence of the place; and for a moment he imagined himself far away in the broad prairies of the West, and lying beneath the luxuriant trees that overhang the banks of the Wabash and the Kaskaskia. He saw the sturgeon leap from the river, and flash for a moment in the sunshine. Then a flock of wild fowl flew across the sky towards the sea mist that was rising slowly in the east; and his soul seemed to float away on the river's current, till he had glided far out into the measureless sea, and the sound of the wind among the leaves was no longer the sound of the wind, but of the sea.

Nature had made Mr. Churchill a poet, but destiny made him

a schoolmaster. This produced a discord between his outward and his inward existence. Life presented itself to him like the Sphinx, with its perpetual riddle of the real and the ideal. To the solution of this dark problem he devoted his days and his nights. He was forced to teach grammar when he would fain have written poems; and from day to day, and from year to year, the trivial things of life postponed the great designs, which he felt capable of accomplishing, but never had the resolute courage to begin. Thus he dallied with his thoughts and with all things, and wasted his strength on trifles; like the lazy sea, that plays with the pebbles on its beach, but under the inspiration of the wind might lift great navies on its outstretched palms, and toss them into the air as playthings.

The evening came. The setting sun stretched his celestial rods of light across the level landscape, and, like the Hebrew in Egypt, smote the rivers and the brooks and the ponds, and they became as blood.

Mr. Churchill turned his steps homeward. He climbed the hill with the old windmill on its summit, and below him saw the lights of the village; and around him the great landscape sinking deeper and deeper into the sea of darkness. He passed an orchard. The air was filled with the odor of the fallen fruit, which seemed to him as sweet as the fragrance of the blossoms in June. A few steps farther brought him to an old and neglected churchyard; and he paused a moment to look at the white gleaming stone, under which slumbered the old clergyman, who came into the village in the time of the Indian wars, and on which was recorded that for half a century he had been "a painful preacher of the word." He entered the village street, and interchanged a few words with Mr. Pendexter, the venerable divine, whom he found standing at his gate. He met, also, an ill-looking man, carrying so many old boots that he seemed literally buried in them; and at intervals encountered a stream of strong tobacco smoke, exhaled from the pipe of an Irish laborer, and pervading the damp evening air. At length he reached his own door.

II

WHEN Mr. Churchill entered his study, he found the lamp lighted, and his wife waiting for him. The wood fire was singing on the hearth like a grasshopper in the heat and silence of a summer noon; and to his heart the chill autumnal evening became a summer noon. His wife turned towards him with looks of love in her joyous blue eyes; and in the serene expression of her face he read the Divine beatitude, "Blessed are the pure in heart."

No sooner had he seated himself by the fireside than the door was swung wide open, and on the threshold stood, with his legs apart, like a miniature colossus, a lovely, golden boy, about three years old, with long, light locks, and very red cheeks. After a moment's pause, he dashed forward into the room with a shout, and established himself in a large armchair, which he converted into a carrier's wagon, and over the back of which he urged forward his imaginary horses. He was followed by Lucy, the maid of all work, bearing in her arms the baby, with large, round eyes, and no hair. In his mouth he held an India rubber ring, and looked very much like a street door knocker. He came down to say good night, but after he got down, could not say it; not being able to say anything but a kind of explosive "Papa!" He was then a good deal kissed and tormented in various ways, and finally sent off to bed blowing little bubbles with his mouth,—Lucy blessing his little heart, and asseverating that nobody could feed him in the night without loving him; and that if the flies bit him any more she would pull out every tooth in their heads!

Then came Master Alfred's hour of triumph and sovereign sway. The firelight gleamed on his hard, red cheeks, and glanced from his liquid eyes, and small, white teeth. He piled his wagon full of books and papers, and dashed off to town at the top of his speed; he delivered and received parcels and letters, and played the postboy's horn with his lips. Then he climbed the back of the great chair, sang "Sweep ho!" as from the top of a very high chimney, and, sliding down upon the cushion, pretended to fall asleep in a little white bed, with white curtains; from which imaginary slumber his father awoke him by crying in his ear, in mysterious tones,—

"What little boy is this!"

Finally he sat down in his chair at his mother's knee, and listened very attentively, and for the hundredth time, to the story of the dog Jumper, which was no sooner ended, than vociferously called for again and again. On the fifth repetition, it was cut as short as the dog's tail by Lucy, who, having put the baby to bed, now came for Master Alfred. He seemed to hope he had been forgotten, but was nevertheless marched off to bed, without any particular regard to his feelings, and disappeared in a kind of abstracted mood, repeating softly to himself his father's words,—

"Good night, Alfred!"

His father looked fondly after him as he went up stairs, holding Lucy by one hand, and with the other rubbing the sleep out of his eyes.

"Ah! these children, these children!" said Mr. Churchill, as he sat down at the tea table; "we ought to love them very much now, for we shall not have them long with us!"

"Good heavens!" exclaimed his wife, "what do you mean? Does anything ail them? Are they going to die?"

"I hope not. But they are going to grow up, and be no longer children."

"O, you foolish man! You gave me such a fright!"

"And yet it seems impossible that they should ever grow to be men, and drag the heavy artillery along the dusty roads of life."

"And I hope they never will. That is the last thing I want either of them to do."

"O, I do not mean literally, only figuratively. By the way, speaking of growing up and growing old, I saw Mr. Pendexter this evening, as I came home."

"And what had he to say?"

"He told me he should preach his farewell sermon tomorrow."

"Poor old man! I really pity him."

"So do I. But it must be confessed he is a dull preacher; and I dare say it is as dull work for him as for his hearers."

"Why are they going to send him away?"

"O, there are a great many reasons. He does not give time and attention enough to his sermons and to his parish. He is always at work on his farm; always wants his salary raised; and insists upon his right to pasture his horse in the parish fields."

"Hark!" cried his wife, lifting up her face in a listening attitude.

"What is the matter?"

"I thought I heard the baby!"

There was a short silence. Then Mr. Churchill said,—

"It was only the cat in the cellar."

At this moment Lucy came in. She hesitated a little, and then, in a submissive voice, asked leave to go down to the village to buy some ribbon for her bonnet. Lucy was a girl of fifteen, who had been taken a few years before from an orphan asylum. Her dark eyes had a gypsy look, and she wore her brown hair twisted round her head after the manner of some of Murillo's girls. She had Milesian blood in her veins, and was impetuous and impatient of contradiction.

When she had left the room, the schoolmaster resumed the conversation by saying,—

"I do not like Lucy's going out so much in the evening. I am afraid she will get into trouble. She is really very pretty."

Then there was another pause, after which he added,—

"My dear wife, one thing puzzles me exceedingly."

"And what is that?"

"It is to know what that man does with all the old boots he picks up about the village. I met him again this evening. He seemed to have as many feet as Briareus had hands. He is a kind of centipede."

"But what has that to do with Lucy?"

"Nothing. It only occurred to me at the moment; and I never can imagine what he does with so many old boots."

III

WHEN tea was over, Mr. Churchill walked to and fro in his study, as his custom was. And as he walked, he gazed with secret rapture at the books, which lined the walls, and thought how many bleeding hearts and aching heads had found consolation for themselves and imparted it to others, by writing those pages. The books seemed to him almost as living beings, so instinct were they with human thoughts and sympathies. It was as if the authors themselves were gazing at him from the walls, with countenances neither sorrowful nor glad, but full of calm indifference to fate, like those of the poets who appeared to Dante in his vision, walking together on the dolorous shore. And then he dreamed of fame, and thought that perhaps hereafter he might be in some degree, and to some one, what these men were to him; and in the enthusiasm of the moment he exclaimed aloud,—

"Would you have me be like these, dear Mary?"

"Like these what?" asked his wife, not comprehending him.

"Like these great and good men,—like these scholars and poets,—the authors of all these books!"

She pressed his hand and said, in a soft, but excited tone,—

"O, yes! Like them, only perhaps better!"

"Then I will write a Romance!"

"Write it!" said his wife, like the angel. For she believed that then he would become famous forever; and that all the vexed and busy world would stand still to hear him blow his little trumpet, whose sound was to rend the adamantine walls of time, and reach the ears of a far-off and startled posterity.

IV

"I was thinking today," said Mr. Churchill a few minutes afterwards, as he took some papers from a drawer scented with a quince, and arranged them on the study table, while his wife as usual seated herself opposite to him with her work in her hand,—"I was thinking today how dull and prosaic the study of mathematics is made in our schoolbooks; as if the grand science of numbers had been discovered and perfected merely to further the purpose of trade."

"For my part," answered his wife, "I do not see how you can make mathematics poetical. There is no poetry in them."

"Ah, that is a very great mistake! There is something divine in the science of numbers. Like God, it holds the sea in the hollow of its hand. It measures the earth; it weighs the stars; it illumines the universe; it is law, it is order, it is beauty. And yet we imagine—that is, most of us—that its highest end and culminating point is bookkeeping by double entry. It is our way of teaching it that makes it so prosaic."

So saying, he arose, and went to one of his bookcases, from the shelf of which he took down a little old quarto volume, and laid it upon the table.

"Now here," he continued, "is a book of mathematics of quite a different stamp from ours."

"It looks very old. What is it?"

"It is the Lilawati of Bhascara Acharya, translated from the Sanscrit."

"It is a pretty name. Pray what does it mean?"

"Lilawati was the name of Bhascara's daughter; and the book was written to perpetuate it. Here is an account of the whole matter."

He then opened the volume, and read as follows:—

"It is said that the composing of Lilawati was occasioned by the following circumstance. Lilawati was the name of the author's daughter, concerning whom it appeared, from the qualities of the ascendant at her birth, that she was destined to pass her life unmarried, and to remain without children. The father ascertained a lucky hour for contracting her in marriage, that she might be firmly connected, and have children. It is said that, when that hour approached, he brought his daughter and his intended son near him. He left the hourcup on the vessel of water, and kept in attendance a time-knowing astrologer, in order that, when the cup should subside in the water, those two precious jewels should be united. But as the intended arrangement was not according to destiny, it happened that the girl, from a curiosity natural to children, looked into the cup to observe the water coming in at the hole; when by chance a pearl separated from her bridal dress, fell into the cup, and, rolling down to the hole, stopped the influx of the water. So the astrologer waited in expectation of the promised hour. When the operation of the cup had thus been delayed beyond all moderate time, the father was in consternation, and examining, he found that a small pearl had stopped the course of the water, and the long-expected hour was passed. In short, the father, thus disappointed, said to his unfortunate daughter, I will write a book of your name, which shall remain to the latest times,— for a good name is a second life, and the groundwork of eternal existence."

As the schoolmaster read, the eyes of his wife dilated and grew tender, and she said,—

"What a beautiful story! When did it happen?"

"Seven hundred years ago, among the Hindoos."

"Why not write a poem about it?"

"Because it is already a poem of itself,—one of those things, of which the simplest statement is the best, and which lose by embellishment. The old Hindoo legend, brown with age, would not please me so well if decked in gay colors, and hung round with the tinkling bells of rhyme. Now hear how the book begins."

Again he read;—

"Salutation to the elephant-headed Being who infuses joy into the minds of his worshippers, who delivers from every difficulty those that call upon him, and whose feet are reverenced by the gods!—Reverence to Ganesa, who is beautiful as the pure purple lotos, and around whose neck the black curling snake winds itself in playful folds!"

"That sounds rather mystical," said his wife.

"Yes, the book begins with a salutation to the Hindoo deities, as the old Spanish Chronicles begin in the name of God, and the Holy Virgin. And now see how poetical some of the examples are."

He then turned over the leaves slowly and read,—

"One-third of a collection of beautiful water lilies is offered to Mahadev, one-fifth to Huri, one-sixth to the Sun, one-fourth to Devi, and six which remain are presented to the spiritual teacher. Required the whole number of water lilies."

"That is very pretty," said the wife, "and would put it into the boys' heads to bring you pond lilies."

"Here is a prettier one still. One-fifth of a hive of bees flew to the Kadamba flower; one-third flew to the Silandhara; three times the difference of these two numbers flew to an arbor; and one bee continued flying about, attracted on each side by the fragrant Ketaki and the Malati. What was the number of the bees?"

"I am sure I should never be able to tell."

"Ten times the square root of a flock of geese——"

Here Mrs. Churchill laughed aloud; but he continued very gravely,—

"Ten times the square root of a flock of geese, seeing the clouds collect, flew to the Manus lake; one-eighth of the whole flew from the edge of the water amongst a multitude of water lilies; and three couple were observed playing in the water. Tell me, my young girl with beautiful locks, what was the whole number of geese?"

"Well, what was it?"

"What should you think?"

"About twenty."

"No, one hundred and forty-four. Now try another. The square root of half a number of bees, and also eight-ninths of the whole, alighted on the jasmines, and a female bee buzzed responsive to the hum of the male enclosed at night in a water lily. O, beautiful damsel, tell me the number of bees."

"That is not there. You made it."

"No, indeed I did not. I wish I had made it. Look and see."

He showed her the book, and she read it herself. He then proposed some of the geometrical questions.

"In a lake the bud of a water lily was observed, one span above the water, and when moved by the gentle breeze, it sunk in the water at two cubits' distance. Required the depth of the water."

"That is charming, but must be very difficult. I could not answer it."

"A tree one hundred cubits high is distant from a well two hundred cubits; from this tree one monkey descends and goes to the well; another monkey takes a leap upwards, and then descends by the hypotenuse; and both pass over an equal space. Required the height of the leap."

"I do not believe you can answer that question yourself, without looking into the book," said the laughing wife, laying her hand over the solution. "Try it."

"With great pleasure, my dear child," cried the confident

schoolmaster, taking a pencil and paper. After making a few figures and calculations, he answered,—

"There, my young girl with beautiful locks, there is the answer,—forty cubits."

His wife removed her hand from the book, and then, clapping both in triumph, she exclaimed,—

"No, you are wrong, you are wrong, my beautiful youth with a bee in your bonnet. It is fifty cubits!"

"Then I must have made some mistake."

"Of course you did. Your monkey did not jump high enough."

She signalized his mortifying defeat as if it had been a victory, by showering kisses, like roses, upon his forehead and cheeks, as he passed beneath the triumphal archway of her arms, trying in vain to articulate,—

"My dearest Lilawati, what is the whole number of the geese?"

V

AFTER extricating himself from this pleasing dilemma, he said,—

"But I am now going to write. I must really begin in sober earnest, or I shall never get anything finished. And you know I have so many things to do, so many books to write, that really I do not know where to begin. I think I will take up the Romance first."

"It will not make much difference, if you only begin!"

"That is true. I will not lose a moment."

"Did you answer Mr. Cartwright's letter about the cottage bedstead?"

"Dear me, no! I forgot it entirely. That must be done first, or he will make it all wrong."

"And the young lady who sent you the poetry to look over and criticize?"

"No; I have not had a single moment's leisure. And there is Mr. Hanson, who wants to know about the cooking range. Confound it! there is always something interfering with my Romance. However, I will despatch those matters very speedily."

And he began to write with great haste. For a while nothing was heard but the scratching of his pen. Then he said, probably in connection with the cooking range,—

"One of the most convenient things in housekeeping is a ham. It is always ready, and always welcome. You can eat it with anything and without anything. It reminds me always of the great wild boar Scrimner, in the Northern Mythology, who is killed every day for the gods to feast on in Valhalla, and comes to life again every night."

"In that case, I should think the gods would have the nightmare," said his wife.

"Perhaps they do."

And then another long silence, broken only by the skating of the swift pen over the sheet. Presently Mrs. Churchill said,—as if following out her own train of thought, while she ceased plying her needle to bite off the thread, which ladies will sometimes do in spite of all that is said against it,—

"A man came here today, calling himself the agent of an extensive house in the needle trade. He left this sample, and said the drill of the eye was superior to any other, and they are warranted not to cut the thread. He puts them at the wholesale price; and if I do not like the sizes, he offers to exchange them for others, either sharps or betweens."

To this remark the abstracted schoolmaster vouchsafed no reply. He found his half-dozen letters not so easily answered, particularly that to the poetical young lady, and worked away busily at them. Finally they were finished and sealed; and he looked up to his wife. She turned her eyes dreamily upon him. Slumber was hanging in their blue orbs, like snow in the heavens, ready to fall. It was quite late, and he said to her,—

"I am too tired, my charming Lilawati, and you too sleepy, to sit here any longer tonight. And, as I do not wish to begin my Romance without having you at my side, so that I can read detached passages to you as I write, I will put it off till tomorrow or the next day."

He watched his wife as she went up stairs with the light. It was a picture always new and always beautiful, and like a painting of Gherardo della Notte. As he followed her, he paused to look at the stars. The beauty of the heavens made his soul overflow.

"How absolute," he exclaimed, "how absolute and omnipotent is the silence of the night! And yet the stillness seems almost audible! From all the measureless depths of air around us comes a half-sound, a half-whisper, as if we could hear the crumbling and falling away of earth and all created things, in the great miracle of nature, decay and reproduction, ever beginning, never ending,—the gradual lapse and running of the sand in the great hourglass of Time!"

In the night, Mr. Churchill had a singular dream. He thought himself in school, where he was reading Latin to his pupils. Suddenly all the genitive cases of the first declension began to make faces at him, and to laugh immoderately; and when he tried to lay hold of them, they jumped down into the ablative, and the circumflex accent assumed the form of a great moustache. Then the little village schoolhouse was transformed into a vast and endless schoolhouse of the world, stretching forward, form after form, through all the generations of coming time; and on all the forms sat young men and old, reading and transcribing his Romance, which now in his dream was completed, and smiling and passing it onward from one to another, till at last the clock in the corner struck twelve, and the weights ran down with a strange, angry whirr, and the school broke up; and the schoolmaster awoke to find this vision of fame only a dream, out of which his alarm clock had aroused him at an untimely hour.

VI

Meanwhile, a different scene was taking place at the parsonage. Mr. Pendexter had retired to his study to finish his farewell sermon. Silence reigned through the house. Sunday had already commenced there. The week ended with the setting of the sun, and the evening and the morning were the first day.

The clergyman was interrupted in his labors by the old sexton, who called as usual for the key of the church. He was gently rebuked for coming so late, and excused himself by saying that his wife was worse.

"Poor woman!" said Mr. Pendexter; "has she her mind?"

"Yes," answered the sexton, "as much as ever."

"She has been ill a long time," continued the clergyman. "We have had prayers for her a great many Sundays."

"It is very true, sir," replied the sexton, mournfully; "I have given you a great deal of trouble. But you need not pray for her any more. It is of no use."

Mr. Pendexter's mind was in too fervid a state to notice the extreme and hopeless humility of his old parishioner, and the unintentional allusion to the inefficacy of his prayers. He pressed the old man's hand warmly, and said, with much emotion,—

"Tomorrow is the last time that I shall preach in this parish, where I have preached for twenty-five years. But it is not the last time I shall pray for you and your family."

The sexton retired also much moved; and the clergyman again resumed his task. His heart glowed and burned within him. Often his face flushed and his eyes filled with tears, so that he could not go on. Often he rose and paced the chamber to and fro, and wiped away the large drops that stood on his red and feverish forehead.

At length the sermon was finished. He rose and looked out of the window. Slowly the clock struck twelve. He had not heard it strike before, since six. The moonlight silvered the distant hills, and lay, white almost as snow, on the frosty roofs of the village. Not a light could be seen at any window.

"Ungrateful people! Could you not watch with me one hour?" exclaimed he, in that excited and bitter moment; as if he had thought that on that solemn night the whole parish would have watched, while he was writing his farewell discourse. He pressed his hot brow against the window pane to allay its fever; and across the tremulous wavelets of the river the tranquil moon sent towards him a silvery shaft of light, like an angelic salutation. And the consoling thought came to him, that not only this river, but all rivers and lakes, and the great sea itself, were flashing with this heavenly light, though he beheld it as a single ray only; and that what to him were the dark waves were the dark providences of God, luminous to others, and even to himself should he change his position.

VII

THE morning came; the dear, delicious, silent Sunday; to the weary workman, both of brain and hand, the beloved day of rest. When the first bell rang, like a brazen mortar, it seemed from its gloomy fortress to bombard the village with bursting shells of sound, that exploded over the houses, shattering the ears of all the parishioners and shaking the consciences of many.

Mr. Pendexter was to preach his farewell sermon. The church was crowded, and only one person came late. It was a modest, meek girl, who stole silently up one of the side aisles,—not so silently, however, but that the pew door creaked a little as she opened it; and straightway a hundred heads were turned in that direction, although it was in the midst of the prayer. Old Mrs. Fairfield did not turn round, but she and her daughter looked at each other, and their bonnets made a parenthesis in the prayer, within which one asked what that was, and the other replied,—

"It is only Alice Archer. She always comes late."

Finally the long prayer was ended, and the congregation sat down, and the weary children—who are always restless during prayers, and had been for nearly half an hour twisting and turning, and standing first on one foot and then on the other, and hanging their heads over the backs of the pews, like tired colts looking into neighboring pastures—settled suddenly down, and subsided into something like rest.

The sermon began,—such a sermon as had never been preached, or even heard of before. It brought many tears into the eyes of the pastor's friends, and made the stoutest hearts among his foes quake with something like remorse. As he announced the text, "Yea, I think it meet as long as I am in this tabernacle to stir you up, by putting you in remembrance," it seemed as if the apostle Peter himself, from whose pen the words first proceeded, were calling them to judgment.

He began by giving a minute sketch of his ministry and the state of the parish, with all its troubles and dissensions, social, political, and ecclesiastical. He concluded by thanking those ladies who had presented him with a black silk gown, and had been kind to his wife during her long illness;—by apologizing for having neglected his own business, which was to study and preach, in order to attend to that of the parish, which was to support its minister,—stating that his own shortcomings had been owing to theirs, which had driven him into the woods in winter and into the fields in summer;—and finally by telling the congregation in general that they were so confirmed in their bad habits, that no reformation was to be expected in them under his ministry, and that to produce one would require a greater exercise of Divine power than it did to create the world; for in creating the world there had been no opposition, whereas, in their reformation, their own obstinacy and evil propensities, and self-seeking, and worldly-mindedness, were all to be overcome!

VIII

WHEN Mr. Pendexter had finished his discourse, and pronounced his last benediction upon a congregation to whose spiritual wants he had ministered for so many years, his people, now his no more, returned home in very various states of mind. Some were exasperated, others mortified, and others filled with pity.

Among the last was Alice Archer,—a fair, delicate girl, whose whole life had been saddened by a too sensitive organization, and by somewhat untoward circumstances. She had a pale, transparent complexion, and large gray eyes, that seemed to see visions. Her figure was slight, almost fragile; her hands white, slender, diaphanous. With these external traits her character was in unison. She was thoughtful, silent, susceptible; often sad, often in tears, often lost in reveries. She led a lonely life with her mother, who was old, querulous, and nearly blind. She had herself inherited a predisposition to blindness; and in her disease there was this peculiarity, that she could see in summer, but in winter the power of vision failed her.

The old house they lived in, with its four sickly Lombardy poplars in front, suggested gloomy and mournful thoughts. It was one of those houses that depress you as you enter, as if many persons had died in it,—sombre, desolate, silent. The very clock in the hall had a dismal sound, gasping and catching its breath at times, and striking the hour with a violent, determined blow, reminding one of Jael driving the nail into the head of Sisera.

One other inmate the house had, and only one. This was Sally Manchester, or Miss Sally Manchester, as she preferred to be called; an excellent chambermaid and a very bad cook, for she served in both capacities. She was, indeed, an extraordinary woman, of large frame and masculine features;—one of those who are born to work, and accept their inheritance of toil as if it were play, and who consequently, in the language of domestic recommendations, are usually styled "a treasure, if you can get her." A treasure she was to this family; for she did all the housework, and in addition took care of the cow and the poultry,—occasionally venturing into the field of veterinary practice, and administering lamp oil to the cock, when she thought he crowed hoarsely. She had on her forehead what is sometimes denominated a "widow's peak,"—that is to say, her hair grew down to a point in the middle; and on Sundays she appeared at church in a blue poplin gown, with a large pink bow on what she called "the congregation side of her bonnet." Her mind was strong, like her person; her disposition not sweet, but, as is sometimes said of apples by way of recommendation, a pleasant sour.

Such were the inmates of the gloomy house,—from which the last-mentioned frequently expressed her intention of retiring, being engaged to a traveling dentist, who, in filling her teeth with amalgam, had seized the opportunity to fill a soft place in her heart with something still more dangerous and mercurial. The wedding day had been from time to time postponed, and at length the family hoped and believed it never would come,— a wish prophetic of its own fulfilment.

Almost the only sunshine that from without shone into the dark mansion came from the face of Cecilia Vaughan, the schoolmate and bosom friend of Alice Archer. They were nearly of the same age, and had been drawn together by that mysterious power which discovers and selects friends for us in our childhood. They sat together in school; they walked together after school; they told each other their manifold secrets; they wrote long and impassioned letters to each other in the evening; in a word, they were in love with each other. It was, so to speak, a rehearsal in girlhood of the great drama of woman's life.

IX

THE golden tints of autumn now brightened the shrubbery around this melancholy house, and took away something of its gloom. The four poplar trees seemed all ablaze, and flickered in the wind like huge torches. The little border of box filled the air with fragrance, and seemed to welcome the return of Alice, as she ascended the steps, and entered the house with a lighter heart than usual. The brisk autumnal air had quickened her pulse and given a glow to her cheek.

She found her mother alone in the parlor, seated in her large armchair. The warm sun streamed in at the uncurtained windows; and lights and shadows from the leaves lay upon her face. She turned her head as Alice entered, and said,—

"Who is it? Is it you, Alice?"

"Yes, it is I, mother."

"Where have you been so long?"

"I have been nowhere, dear mother. I have come directly home from church."

"How long it seems to me! It is very late. It is growing quite dark. I was just going to call for the lights."

"Why, mother!" exclaimed Alice, in a startled tone; "what do you mean? The sun is shining directly into your face!"

"Impossible, my dear Alice. It is quite dark. I cannot see you. Where are you?"

She leaned over her mother and kissed her. Both were silent,—both wept. They knew that the hour, so long looked forward to with dismay, had suddenly come. Mrs. Archer was blind!

This scene of sorrow was interrupted by the abrupt entrance of Sally Manchester. She, too, was in tears; but she was weeping for her own affliction. In her hand she held an open letter, which she gave to Alice, exclaiming amid sobs,—

"Read this, Miss Archer, and see how false man can be! Never trust any man! They are all alike; they are all false—false—false!"

Alice took the letter and read as follows:—

"It is with pleasure, Miss Manchester, I sit down to write you a few lines. I esteem you as highly as ever, but Providence has seemed to order and direct my thoughts and affections to another,—one in my own neighborhood. It was rather unexpected to me. Miss Manchester, I suppose you are well aware that we, as professed Christians, ought to be resigned to our lot in this world. May God assist you, so that we may be prepared to join the great company in heaven. Your answer would be very desirable. I respect your virtue, and regard you as a friend.

MARTIN CHERRYFIELD.

"P. S. The society is generally pretty good here, but the state of religion is quite low."

"That is a cruel letter, Sally," said Alice, as she handed it back to her. "But we all have our troubles. That man is unworthy of you. Think no more about him."

"What is the matter?" inquired Mrs. Archer, hearing the counsel given and the sobs with which it was received. "Sally, what is the matter?"

Sally made no answer; but Alice said,—

"Mr. Cherryfield has fallen in love with somebody else."

"Is that all?" said Mrs. Archer, evidently relieved. "She ought to be very glad of it. Why does she want to be married? She had much better stay with us; particularly now that I am blind."

When Sally heard this last word, she looked up in consternation. In a moment she forgot her own grief to sympathize with Alice and her mother. She wanted to do a thousand things at once;—to go here;—to send there;—to get this and that;—and particularly to call all the doctors in the neighborhood. Alice assured her it would be of no avail, though she finally consented that one should be sent for.

Sally went in search of him. On her way, her thoughts reverted to herself; and, to use her own phrase, "she curbed in like a stage horse," as she walked. This state of haughty and offended pride continued for some hours after her return home. Later in the day, she assumed a decent composure, and requested that the man—she scorned to name him—might never again be mentioned in her hearing. Thus was her whole dream of felicity swept away by the tide of fate, as the nest of a ground swallow by an inundation. It had been built too low to be secure.

Some women, after a burst of passionate tears, are soft, gentle, affectionate; a warm and genial air succeeds the rain. Others clear up cold, and are breezy, bleak, and dismal. Of the latter class was Sally Manchester. She became embittered against all men on account of one; and was often heard to say that she thought women were fools to be married, and that, for one, she would not marry any man, let him be who he might,—not she!

The village doctor came. He was a large man, of the cheerful kind; vigorous, florid, encouraging; and pervaded by an indiscriminate odor of drugs. Loud voice, large cane, thick boots; —everything about him synonymous with noise. His presence in the sickroom was like martial music,—inspiriting, but loud. He seldom left it without saying to the patient, "I hope you will feel more comfortable tomorrow," or, "When your fever leaves you, you will be better." But, in this instance, he could not go so far. Even his hopefulness was not sufficient for the emergency. Mrs. Archer was blind,—beyond remedy, beyond hope,—irrevocably blind!

X

On the following morning, very early, as the schoolmaster stood at his door, inhaling the bright, wholesome air, and beholding the shadows of the rising sun, and the flashing dewdrops on the red vine leaves, he heard the sound of wheels, and saw Mr. Pendexter and his wife drive down the village street in their old-fashioned chaise, known by all the boys in town as "the ark." The old white horse, that for so many years had stamped at funerals, and gnawed the tops of so many posts, and imagined he killed so many flies because he wagged the stump of a tail, and, finally, had been the cause of so much discord in the parish, seemed now to make common cause with his master, and stepped as if endeavoring to shake the dust from his feet as he passed out of the ungrateful village. Under the axletree hung suspended a leather trunk; and in the chaise, between the two occupants, was a large bandbox, which forced Mr. Pendexter to let his legs hang out of the vehicle, and gave him the air of imitating the scriptural behavior of his horse. Gravely and from a distance he saluted the schoolmaster, who saluted him in return, with a tear in his eye, that no man saw, but which, nevertheless, was not unseen.

"Farewell, poor old man!" said the schoolmaster within himself, as he shut out the cold autumnal air, and entered his comfortable study. "We are not worthy of thee, or we should have had thee with us forever. Go back again to the place of thy childhood, the scene of thine early labors and thine early love; let thy days end where they began, and like the emblem of eternity, let the serpent of life coil itself round and take its tail into its mouth, and be still from all its hissings for evermore! I would not call thee back; for it is better thou shouldst be where thou art, than amid the angry contentions of this little town."

Not all took leave of the old clergyman in so kindly a spirit. Indeed, there was a pretty general feeling of relief in the village, as when one gets rid of an ill-fitting garment, or old-fashioned hat, which one neither wishes to wear, nor is quite willing to throw away.

Thus Mr. Pendexter departed from the village. A few days afterwards he was seen at a fall training, or general muster of the militia, making a prayer on horseback, with his eyes wide open; a performance in which he took evident delight, as it gave him an opportunity of going quite at large into some of the bloodiest campaigns of the ancient Hebrews.

XI

For a while the schoolmaster walked to and fro, looking at the gleam of the sunshine on the carpet, and reveling in his daydreams of unwritten books, and literary fame. With these daydreams mingled confusedly the pattering of little feet, and the murmuring and cooing of his children overhead. His plans that morning, could he have executed them, would have filled a shelf in his library with poems and romances of his own creation. But suddenly the vision vanished; and another from the actual world took its place. It was the canvas-covered cart of the butcher, that, like the flying wigwam of the Indian tale, flitted before his eyes. It drove up the yard and stopped at the back door; and the poet felt that the sacred rest of Sunday, the God's-truce with worldly cares, was once more at an end. A dark hand passed between him and the land of light. Suddenly closed the ivory gate of dreams, and the horn gate of every-day life opened, and he went forth to deal with the man of flesh and blood.

"Alas!" said he with a sigh; "and must my life, then, always be like the Sabbatical river of the Jews, flowing in full stream only on the seventh day, and sandy and arid all the rest?"

Then he thought of his beautiful wife and children, and added, half aloud,—

"No; not so! Rather let me look upon the seven days of the week as the seven magic rings of Jarchas, each inscribed with the name of a separate planet, and each possessing a peculiar power;—or as the seven sacred and mysterious stones which the pilgrims of Mecca were forced to throw over their shoulders in the valleys of Menah and Akbah, cursing the devil and saying at each throw, 'God is great!'"

He found Mr. Wilmerdings, the butcher, standing beside his cart, and surrounded by five cats, that had risen simultaneously on their hind legs, to receive their quotidian morning's meal. Mr. Wilmerdings not only supplied the village with fresh provisions daily, but he likewise weighed all the babies. There was hardly a child in town that had not hung beneath his steelyards, tied in a silk handkerchief, the movable weight above sliding along the notched beam from eight pounds to twelve. He was a young man with a very fresh and rosy complexion, and every Monday morning he appeared dressed in an exceedingly white frock. He had lately married a milliner, who sold "Dunstable and eleven-braid, openwork and colored straws," and their bridal tour had been to a neighboring town to see a man hanged for murdering his wife. A pair of huge ox horns branched from the gable of his slaughterhouse; and near it stood the great pits of the tannery, which all the schoolboys thought were filled with blood!

Perhaps no two men could be more unlike than Mr. Churchill and Mr. Wilmerdings. Upon such a grating, iron hinge opened the door of his daily life;—opened into the schoolroom, the theatre of those lifelong labors, which theoretically are the most noble, and practically the most vexatious in the world. Toward this, as soon as breakfast was over, and he had played awhile with his children, he directed his steps. On his way, he had many glimpses into the lovely realms of Nature, and one into those of Art, through the medium of a placard pasted against a wall. It was as follows:—

"The subscriber professes to take profiles, plain and shaded, which, viewed at right angles with the serious countenance, are warranted to be infallibly correct.

"No trouble of adorning or dressing the person is required. He takes infants and children at sight, and has frames of all sizes to accommodate.

"A profile is a delineated outline of the exterior form of any person's face and head, the use of which when seen tends to vivify the affections of those whom we esteem or love.

WILLIAM BANTAM."

Ere long even this glimpse into the ideal world had vanished; and he felt himself bound to the earth with a hundred invisible threads, by which a hundred urchins were tugging and tormenting him; and it was only with considerable effort, and at intervals, that his mind could soar to the moral dignity of his profession.

Such was the schoolmaster's life; and a dreary, weary life it would have been, had not poetry from within gushed through every crack and crevice in it. This transformed it, and made it resemble a well, into which stones and rubbish have been thrown; but underneath is a spring of fresh, pure water, which nothing external can ever check or defile.

XII

Mr. Pendexter had departed. Only a few old and middle-aged people regretted him. To these few, something was wanting in the service ever afterwards. They missed the accounts of the Hebrew massacres, and the wonderful tales of the Zumzum-mims; they missed the venerable gray hair, and the voice that had spoken to them in childhood, and forever preserved the memory of it in their hearts, as in the Russian church the old hymns of the earliest centuries are still piously retained.

The winter came, with all its affluence of snows, and its many candidates for the vacant pulpit. But the parish was difficult to please, as all parishes are; and talked of dividing itself, and building a new church, and other extravagances, as all parishes do. Finally it concluded to remain as it was, and the choice of a pastor was made.

The events of the winter were few in number, and can be easily described. The following extract from a schoolgirl's letter to an absent friend contains the most important:—

"At school, things have gone on pretty much as usual. Jane Brown has grown very pale. They say she is in a consumption; but I think it is because she eats so many slate pencils. One of her shoulders has grown a good deal higher than the other. Billy Wilmerdings has been turned out of school for playing truant. He promised his mother, if she would not whip him, he would experience religion. I am sure I wish he would; for then he would stop looking at me through the hole in the top of his desk. Mr. Churchill is a very curious man. Today he gave us this question in arithmetic: 'One-fifth of a hive of bees flew to the Kadamba flower; one-third flew to the Silandhara; three times the difference of these two numbers flew to an arbor; and one bee continued flying about, attracted on each side by the fragrant Ketaki and the Malati. What was the number of bees?' Nobody could do the sum.

"The church has been repaired, and we have a new mahogany pulpit. Mr. Churchill bought the old one, and had it put up in his study. What a strange man he is! A good many candidates have preached for us. The only one we like is Mr. Kavanagh. Arthur Kavanagh! is not that a romantic name? He is tall, very pale, with beautiful black eyes and hair! Sally—Alice Archer's Sally—says 'he is not a man; he is a Thaddeus of Warsaw!' I think he is very handsome. And such sermons! So beautifully written, so different from old Mr. Pendexter's! He has been invited to settle here; but he cannot come till spring. Last Sunday he preached about the ruling passion. He said that once a German nobleman, when he was dying, had his hunting horn blown in his bedroom, and his hounds let in, springing and howling about him; and that so it was with the ruling passions of men; even around the deathbed, at the well-known signal, they howled and leaped about those that had fostered them! Beautiful, is it not? and so original! He said in another sermon, that disappointments feed and nourish us in the desert places of life, as the ravens did the Prophet in the wilderness; and that as, in Catholic countries, the lamps lighted before the images of saints, in narrow and dangerous streets, not only served as offerings of devotion, but likewise as lights to those who passed, so, in the dark and dismal streets of the city of Unbelief, every good thought, word, and deed of a man, not only was an offering to heaven, but likewise served to light him and others on their way homeward! I have taken a good many notes of Mr. Kavanagh's sermons, which you shall see when you come back.

"Last week we had a sleigh ride, with six white horses. We went like the wind over the hollows in the snow;—the driver called them 'thank-you-ma'ams,' because they make everybody bow. And such a frantic ball as we had at Beaverstock! I wish you had been there! We did not get home till two o'clock in the morning; and the next day Hester Green's minister asked her if she did not feel the fire of a certain place growing hot under her feet, while she was dancing!

"The new fashionable boarding school begins next week. The prospectus has been sent to our house. One of the regulations is, 'Young ladies are not allowed to cross their benders in school'! Papa says he never heard them called so before. Old Mrs. Plainfield is gone at last. Just before she died, her Irish chambermaid asked her if she wanted to be buried with her false teeth in! There has not been a single new engagement since you went away. But somebody asked me the other day if you were engaged to Mr. Pillsbury. I was very angry. Pillsbury, indeed! He is old enough to be your father!

"What a long, rambling letter I am writing you!—and only because you will be so naughty as to stay away and leave me all alone. If you could have seen the moon last night! But what a goose I am!—as if you did not see it! Was it not glorious? You cannot imagine, dearest, how every hour in the day I wish you were here with me. I know you would sympathize with all my feelings, which Hester does not at all. For, if I admire the moon, she says I am romantic, and, for her part, if there is any thing she despises, it is the moon! and that she prefers a snug, warm bed (O, horrible!) to all the moons in the universe!"

XIII

THE events mentioned in this letter were the principal ones that occurred during the winter. The case of Billy Wilmerdings grew quite desperate. In vain did his father threaten and the schoolmaster expostulate; he was only the more sullen and stubborn. In vain did his mother represent to his weary mind, that, if he did not study, the boys who knew the dead languages

would throw stones at him in the street; he only answered that
he should like to see them try it. Till, finally, having lost many
of his illusions, and having even discovered that his father was
not the greatest man in the world, on the breaking up of the
ice in the river, to his own infinite relief and that of the whole
village, he departed on a coasting trip in a fore-and-aft schooner,
which constituted the entire navigation of Fairmeadow.

Mr. Churchill had really put up in his study the old white,
wineglass-shaped pulpit. It served as a playhouse for his
children, who, whether in it or out of it, daily preached to
his heart, and were a living illustration of the way to enter
into the kingdom of heaven. Moreover, he himself made use
of it externally as a notebook, recording his many meditations
with a pencil on the white panels. The following will serve as
a specimen of this pulpit eloquence:—

Morality without religion is only a kind of dead reckoning,—
an endeavor to find our place on a cloudy sea by measuring the
distance we have run, but without any observation of the
heavenly bodies.

Many readers judge of the power of a book by the shock
it gives their feelings,—as some savage tribes determine the
power of muskets by their recoil; that being considered best
which fairly prostrates the purchaser.

Men of genius are often dull and inert in society; as the
blazing meteor, when it descends to earth, is only a stone.

The natural alone is permanent. Fantastic idols may be
worshipped for a while; but at length they are overturned by
the continual and silent progress of Truth, as the grim statues
of Copan have been pushed from their pedestals by the growth
of forest trees, whose seeds were sown by the wind in the
ruined walls.

The everyday cares and duties, which men call drudgery, are
the weights and counterpoises of the clock of time, giving its

pendulum a true vibration, and its hands a regular motion; and when they cease to hang upon the wheels, the pendulum no longer swings, the hands no longer move, the clock stands still.

The same object, seen from the three different points of view, —the Past, the Present, and the Future,—often exhibits three different faces to us; like those signboards over shop doors, which represent the face of a lion as we approach, of a man when we are in front, and of an ass when we have passed.

In character, in manners, in style, in all things, the supreme excellence is simplicity.

With many readers, brilliancy of style passes for affluence of thought; they mistake buttercups in the grass for immeasurable gold mines under ground.

The motives and purposes of authors are not always so pure and high, as, in the enthusiasm of youth, we sometimes imagine. To many the trumpet of fame is nothing but a tin horn to call them home, like laborers from the field, at dinner time; and they think themselves lucky to get the dinner.

The rays of happiness, like those of light, are colorless when unbroken.

Critics are sentinels in the grand army of letters, stationed at the corners of newspapers and reviews, to challenge every new author.

The country is lyric,—the town dramatic. When mingled, they make the most perfect musical drama.

Our passions never wholly die; but in the last cantos of life's romantic epos, they rise up again and do battle, like some of Ariosto's heroes, who have already been quietly interred, and ought to be turned to dust.

This country is not priest ridden, but press ridden.

Some critics have the habit of rowing up the Heliconian rivers with their backs turned, so as to see the landscape precisely as the poet did not see it. Others see faults in a book much larger than the book itself; as Sancho Panza, with his eyes blinded, beheld from his wooden horse the earth no larger than a grain of mustard seed, and the men and women on it as large as hazelnuts.

Like an inundation of the Indus is the course of time. We look for the homes of our childhood, they are gone; for the friends of our childhood, they are gone. The loves and animosities of youth, where are they? Swept away like the camps that had been pitched in the sandy bed of the river.

As no saint can be canonized until the devil's advocate has exposed all his evil deeds, and showed why he should not be made a saint, so no poet can take his station among the gods until the critics have said all that can be said against him.

It is curious to note the old sea margins of human thought! Each subsiding century reveals some new mystery; we build where monsters used to hide themselves.

XIV

AT length the spring came, and brought the birds, and the flowers, and Mr. Kavanagh, the new clergyman, who was ordained with all the pomp and ceremony usual on such occasions. The opening of the season furnished also the theme of his first discourse, which some of the congregation thought very beautiful, and others very incomprehensible.

Ah, how wonderful is the advent of the spring!—the great annual miracle of the blossoming of Aaron's rod, repeated on myriads and myriads of branches!—the gentle progression and growth of herbs, flowers, trees,—gentle, and yet irrepressible,—which no force can stay, no violence restrain, like love, that wins its way and cannot be withstood by any human power, because itself is divine power. If spring came but once in a century, instead of once a year, or burst forth with the sound of an earthquake, and not in silence, what wonder and expectation would there be in all hearts to behold the miraculous change!

But now the silent succession suggests nothing but necessity. To most men, only the cessation of the miracle would be miraculous, and the perpetual exercise of God's power seems less wonderful than its withdrawal would be. We are like children who are astonished and delighted only by the second hand of the clock, not by the hour hand.

Such was the train of thought with which Kavanagh commenced his sermon. And then, with deep solemnity and emotion, he proceeded to speak of the spring of the soul, as from its cheerless wintry distance it turns nearer and nearer to the great sun, and clothes its dry and withered branches anew with leaves and blossoms, unfolded from within itself, beneath the penetrating and irresistible influence.

While delivering the discourse, Kavanagh had not succeeded so entirely in abstracting himself from all outward things as not to note in some degree its effect upon his hearers. As in modern times no applause is permitted in our churches, however moved the audience may be, and, consequently, no one dares wave his hat and shout,—"Orthodox Chrysostom! Thirteenth Apostle! Worthy the Priesthood!"—as was done in the days of the Christian Fathers; and, moreover, as no one after church spoke to him of his sermon, or of any thing else,—he went home with rather a heavy heart, and a feeling of discouragement. One thing had cheered and consoled him. It was the pale countenance of a young girl, whose dark eyes had been fixed upon him during the whole discourse with unflagging interest and attention. She sat alone in a pew near the pulpit. It was Alice Archer. Ah! could he have known how deeply sank his words into that simple heart, he might have shuddered with another kind of fear than that of not moving his audience sufficiently!

XV

ON the following morning Kavanagh sat musing upon his worldly affairs, and upon various little household arrangements which it would be necessary for him to make. To aid him in these, he had taken up the village paper, and was running over the columns of advertisements,—those narrow and crowded thoroughfares, in which the wants and wishes of humanity display themselves like mendicants without disguise. His eye ran hastily over the advantageous offers of the cheap tailors and the dealers in patent medicines. He wished neither to be clothed nor cured. In one place he saw that a young lady, perfectly competent, desired to form a class of young mothers and nurses, and to instruct them in the art of talking to infants so as to interest and amuse them; and in another, that the firemen of Fairmeadow wished well to those hostile editors who had called them gamblers, drunkards, and rioters, and hoped that they might be spared from that great fire which they were told could never be extinguished! Finally his eye rested on the advertisement of a carpet warehouse, in which the one-price system was strictly adhered to. It was farther stated that a discount would be made "to clergymen on small salaries, feeble churches, and charitable institutions." Thinking that this was doubtless the place for one who united in himself two of these qualifications for a discount, with a smile on his lips, he took his hat and sallied forth into the street.

A few days previous, Kavanagh had discovered in the tower of the church a vacant room, which he had immediately determined to take possession of, and to convert into a study. From this retreat, through the four oval windows, fronting the four corners of the heavens, he could look down upon the streets, the roofs and gardens of the village,—on the winding river, the meadows, the farms, the distant blue mountains. Here he could sit and meditate, in that peculiar sense of seclusion and spiritual elevation, that entire separation from the world below, which a chamber in a tower always gives. Here, uninterrupted and aloof from all intrusion, he could pour his heart into those discourses, with which he hoped to reach and move the hearts of his parishioners.

It was to furnish this retreat, that he went forth on the Monday morning after his first sermon. He was not long in procuring the few things needed,—the carpet, the table, the chairs, the shelves for books; and was returning thoughtfully homeward, when his eye was caught by a signboard on the corner of the street, inscribed "Moses Merryweather, Dealer in Singing Birds, Foreign and Domestic." He saw also a whole chamber window transformed into a cage, in which sundry canary birds, and others of gayer plumage, were jargoning together, like people in the marketplaces of foreign towns. At the sight of these old favorites, a long slumbering passion awoke within him; and he straightway ascended the dark wooden staircase, with the intent of enlivening his solitary room with the vivacity and songs of these captive ballad singers.

In a moment he found himself in a little room hung round with cages, roof and walls; full of sunshine; full of twitterings, cooings, and flutterings; full of downy odors, suggesting nests, and dovecots, and distant islands inhabited only by birds. The taxidermist—the Selkirk of the sunny island—was not there; but a young lady of noble mien, who was looking at an English goldfinch in a square cage with a portico, turned upon him, as he entered, a fair and beautiful face, shaded by long, light locks, in which the sunshine seemed entangled, as among the boughs of trees. That face he had never seen before, and yet it seemed familiar to him; and the added light in her large, celestial eyes, and the almost imperceptible expression that passed over her face, showed that she knew who he was.

At the same moment the taxidermist presented himself, coming from an inner room;—a little man in gray, with spectacles upon his nose, holding in his hands, with wings and legs drawn close and smoothly together, like the green husks of the maize ear, a beautiful carrier pigeon, who turned up first one bright eye and then the other, as if asking, "What are you going to do with me now?" This silent inquiry was soon answered by Mr. Merryweather, who said to the young lady,—

"Here, Miss Vaughan, is the best carrier pigeon in my whole collection. The real Columba Tabullaria. He is about three years old, as you can see by his wattle."

"A very pretty bird," said the lady; "and how shall I train it?"

"O, that is very easy. You have only to keep it shut up for a few days, well fed and well treated. Then take it in an open cage to the place you mean it to fly to, and do the same thing there. Afterwards it will give you no trouble; it will always fly between those two places."

"That, certainly, is not very difficult. At all events, I will make the trial. You may send the bird home to me. On what shall I feed it?"

"On any kind of grain,—barley and buckwheat are best; and remember to let it have a plenty of gravel in the bottom of its cage."

"I will not forget. Send me the bird today, if possible."

With these words she departed, much too soon for Kavanagh, who was charmed with her form, her face, her voice; and who, when left alone with the little taxidermist, felt that the momentary fascination of the place was gone. He heard no longer the singing of the birds; he saw no longer their gay plumage; and having speedily made the purchase of a canary and a cage, he likewise departed, thinking of the carrier pigeons of Bagdad, and the columbaries of Egypt, stationed at fixed intervals as relays and resting places for the flying post. With an indefinable feeling of sadness, too, came wafted like a perfume through his memory those tender, melancholy lines of Maria del Occidente:—

"And as the dove, to far Palmyra flying,
    From where her native founts of Antioch beam,
Weary, exhausted, longing, panting, sighing,
    Lights sadly at the desert's bitter stream;

So many a soul, o'er life's drear desert faring,—
    Love's pure, congenial spring unfound, unquaffed,—
Suffers, recoils, then, thirsty and despairing
    Of what it would, descends and sips the nearest draught."

Meanwhile, Mr. Merryweather, left to himself, walked about his aviary, musing, and talking to his birds. Finally he paused before the tin cage of a gray African parrot, between which and himself there was a strong family likeness, and, giving it his finger to peck and perch upon, conversed with it in that peculiar dialect with which it had often made vocal the distant groves of Zanguebar. He then withdrew to the inner room, where he resumed his labor of stuffing a cardinal grossbeak, saying to himself between whiles,—

"I wonder what Miss Cecilia Vaughan means to do with a carrier pigeon!"

Some mysterious connection he had evidently established already between this pigeon and Mr. Kavanagh; for, continuing his reverie, he said, half aloud,—

"Of course she would never think of marrying a poor clergyman!"

XVI

THE old family mansion of the Vaughans stood a little out of town, in the midst of a pleasant farm. The county road was not near enough to annoy; and the rattling wheels and little clouds of dust seemed like friendly salutations from travelers as they passed. They spoke of safety and companionship, and took away all loneliness from the solitude.

On three sides, the farm was enclosed by willow and alder hedges, and the flowing wall of a river; nearer the house were groves clear of all underwood, with rocky knolls, and breezy bowers of beech; and afar off the blue hills broke the horizon, creating secret longings for what lay beyond them, and filling the mind with pleasant thoughts of Prince Rasselas and the Happy Valley.

The house was one of the few old houses still standing in New England;—a large, square building, with a portico in front, whose door in summer time stood open from morning until night. A pleasing stillness reigned about it; and soft gusts of pine-embalmed air, and distant cawings from the crow-haunted mountains, filled its airy and ample halls.

In this old-fashioned house had Cecilia Vaughan grown up to maidenhood. The traveling shadows of the clouds on the hillsides,—the sudden summer wind, that lifted the languid leaves, and rushed from field to field, from grove to grove, the forerunner of the rain,—and, most of all, the mysterious mountain, whose coolness was a perpetual invitation to her, and whose silence a perpetual fear,—fostered her dreamy and poetic temperament. Not less so did the reading of poetry and romance in the long, silent, solitary winter evenings. Her mother had been dead for many years, and the memory of that mother had become almost a religion to her. She recalled it incessantly; and the reverential love, which it inspired, completely filled her soul with melancholy delight. Her father was a kindly old man; a judge in one of the courts; dignified, affable, somewhat bent by his legal erudition, as a shelf is by the weight of the books upon it. His papers encumbered the study table;—his law books, the study floor. They seemed to shut out from his mind the lovely daughter, who had grown up to womanhood by his side, but almost without his recognition. Always affectionate, always indulgent, he left her to walk alone, without his stronger thought and firmer purpose to lean upon; and though her education had been, on this account, somewhat desultory, and her imagination indulged in many dreams and vagaries, yet, on the whole, the result had been more favorable than in many cases where the process of instruction has been too diligently carried on, and where, as sometimes on the roofs of farmhouses and barns, the scaffolding has been left to deform the building.

Cecilia's bosom friend at school was Alice Archer; and, after they left school, the love between them, and consequently the letters, rather increased than diminished. These two young hearts found not only a delight, but a necessity in pouring forth their thoughts and feelings to each other; and it was to facilitate this intercommunication, for whose exigencies the ordinary methods were now found inadequate, that the carrier pigeon had been purchased. He was to be the flying post; their bedrooms the dovecots, the pure and friendly columbaria.

Endowed with youth, beauty, talent, fortune, and, moreover, with that indefinable fascination which has no name, Cecilia Vaughan was not without lovers, avowed and unavowed;—young men, who made an ostentatious display of their affection;—boys, who treasured it in their bosoms, as something indescribably sweet and precious, perfuming all the chambers of the heart with its celestial fragance. Whenever she returned from a visit to the city, some unknown youth of elegant manners and varnished leather boots was sure to hover round the village inn for a few days,—was known to visit the Vaughans assiduously, and then silently to disappear, and be seen no more. Of course, nothing could be known of the secret history of such individuals; but shrewd surmises were formed as to their designs and their destinies; till finally, any well-dressed stranger, lingering in the village without ostensible business, was set down as "one of Miss Vaughan's lovers."

In all this, what a contrast was there between the two young friends! The wealth of one and the poverty of the other were not so strikingly at variance, as this affluence and refluence of love. To the one, so much was given that she became regardless of the gift; from the other, so much withheld, that, if possible, she exaggerated its importance.

XVII

IN addition to these transient lovers, who were but birds of passage, winging their way, in an incredibly short space of time, from the torrid to the frigid zone, there was in the village a domestic and resident adorer, whose love for himself, for Miss Vaughan, and for the beautiful, had transformed his name from Hiram A. Hawkins to H. Adolphus Hawkins. He was a dealer in English linens and carpets;—a profession which of itself fills the mind with ideas of domestic comfort. His waistcoats were made like Lord Melbourne's in the illustrated English papers, and his shiny hair went off to the left in a superb sweep, like the handrail of a bannister. He wore many rings on his fingers, and several breastpins and gold chains disposed about his person. On all his bland physiognomy was stamped, as on some of his linens, "Soft finish for family use." Everything about him spoke the lady's man. He was, in fact, a perfect ringdove; and, like the rest of his species, always walked up to the female, and, bowing his head, swelled out his white crop, and uttered a very plaintive murmur.

Moreover, Mr. Hiram Adolphus Hawkins was a poet,—so much a poet, that, as his sister frequently remarked, he "spoke blank verse in the bosom of his family." The general tone of his productions was sad, desponding, perhaps slightly morbid. How could it be otherwise with the writings of one who had never been the world's friend, nor the world his? who looked upon himself as "a pyramid of mind on the dark desert of despair"? and who, at the age of twenty-five, had drunk the bitter draught of life to the dregs, and dashed the goblet down? His productions were published in the Poet's Corner of the Fairmeadow Advertiser; and it was a relief to know, that, in private life, as his sister remarked, he was "by no means the censorious and moody person some of his writings might imply."

Such was the personage who assumed to himself the perilous position of Miss Vaughan's permanent admirer. He imagined that it was impossible for any woman to look upon him and not love him. Accordingly, he paraded himself at his shop door as she passed; he paraded himself at the corners of the streets; he paraded himself at the church steps on Sunday. He spied her from the window; he sallied from the door; he followed her with his eyes; he followed her with his whole august person; he passed her and repassed her, and turned back to gaze; he lay in wait with dejected countenance and desponding air; he persecuted her with his looks; he pretended that their souls could comprehend each other without words; and whenever her lovers were alluded to in his presence, he gravely declared, as one who had reason to know, that, if Miss Vaughan ever married, it would be some one of gigantic intellect!

Of these persecutions Cecilia was for a long time the unconscious victim. She saw this individual, with rings and strange waistcoats, performing his gyrations before her, but did not suspect that she was the center of attraction,—not imagining that any man would begin his wooing with such outrages. Gradually the truth dawned upon her, and became the source of indescribable annoyance, which was augmented by a series of anonymous letters, written in a female hand, and setting forth the excellences of a certain mysterious relative,—his modesty, his reserve, his extreme delicacy, his talent for poetry,—rendered authentic by extracts from his papers, made, of course, without the slightest knowledge or suspicion on his part. Whence came these sibylline leaves? At first Cecilia could not divine; but, ere long, her woman's instinct traced them to the thin and nervous hand of the poet's sister. This surmise was confirmed by her maid, who asked the boy that brought them.

It was with one of these missives in her hand that Cecilia entered Mrs. Archer's house, after purchasing the carrier pigeon. Unannounced she entered, and walked up the narrow and imperfectly lighted stairs to Alice's bedroom,—that little sanctuary draped with white,—that columbarium lined with warmth, and softness, and silence. Alice was not there; but the chair by the window, the open volume of poems on the table, the note to Cecilia by its side, and the ink not yet dry in the pen, were like the vibration of a bough, when the bird has just left it,—like the rising of the grass, when the foot has just pressed it. In a moment she returned. She had been down to her mother, who sat talking, talking, talking, with an old friend in the parlor below, even as these young friends were talking together, in the bedroom above. Ah, how different were their themes! Death and Love,—apples of Sodom, that crumble to ashes at a touch,—golden fruits of the Hesperides,—golden fruits of Paradise, fragrant, ambrosial, perennial!

"I have just been writing to you," said Alice; "I wanted so much to see you this morning!"

"Why this morning in particular? Has anything happened?"

"Nothing, only I had such a longing to see you!"

And, seating herself in a low chair by Cecilia's side, she laid her head upon the shoulder of her friend, who, taking one of her pale, thin hands in both her own, silently kissed her forehead again and again.

Alice was not aware, that, in the words she uttered, there was the slightest shadow of untruth. And yet had nothing happened? Was it nothing, that among her thoughts a new thought had risen, like a star, whose pale effulgence, mingled with the common daylight, was not yet distinctly visible even to herself, but would grow brighter as the sun grew lower, and the rosy twilight darker? Was it nothing, that a new fountain of affection had suddenly sprung up within her, which she mistook for the freshening and overflowing of the old fountain of friendship, that hitherto had kept the lowland landscape of her life so green, but now, being flooded by more affection, was not to cease, but only to disappear in the greater tide, and flow unseen beneath it? Yet so it was; and this stronger yearning —this unappeasable desire for her friend—was only the tumultuous swelling of a heart, that as yet knows not its own secret.

"I am so glad to see you, Cecilia!" she continued. "You are so beautiful! I love so much to sit and look at you! Ah, how I wish Heaven had made me as tall, and strong, and beautiful as you are!"

"You little flatterer! What an affectionate, lover-like friend you are! What have you been doing all the morning?"

"Looking out of the window, thinking of you, and writing you this letter, to beg you to came and see me."

"And I have been buying a carrier pigeon, to fly between us, and carry all our letters."

"That will be delightful."

"He is to be sent home today; and after he gets accustomed to my room, I shall send him here, to get acquainted with yours;—a Iachimo in my Imogen's bedchamber, to spy out its secrets."

"If he sees Cleopatra in these white curtains, and silver Cupids in these andirons, he will have your imagination."

"He will see the book with the leaf turned down, and you asleep, and tell me all about you."

"A carrier pigeon! What a charming idea! and how like you to think of it!"

"But today I have been obliged to bring my own letters. I have some more sibylline leaves from my anonymous correspondent, in laud and exaltation of her modest relative, who speaks blank verse in the bosom of his family. I have brought them to read you some extracts, and to take your advice; for, really and seriously, this must be stopped. It has grown too annoying."

"How much love you have offered you!" said Alice, sighing.

"Yes, quite too much of this kind. On my way here, I saw the modest relative, standing at the corner of the street, hanging his head in this way."

And she imitated the melancholy Hiram Adolphus, and the young friends laughed.

"I hope you did not notice him?" resumed Alice.

"Certainly not. But what do you suppose he did? As soon as he saw me, he began to walk backward down the street only a short distance in front of me, staring at me most impertinently. Of course, I took no notice of this strange conduct. I felt myself blushing to the eyes with indignation, and yet could hardly suppress my desire to laugh."

"If you had laughed, he would have taken it for an encouragement; and I have no doubt it would have brought on the catastrophe."

"And that would have ended the matter. I half wish I had laughed."

"But think of the immortal glory of marrying a poet!"

"And of inscribing on my cards, Mrs. Hiram Adolphus Hawkins!"

"A few days ago, I went to buy something at his shop; and, leaning over the counter, he asked me if I had seen the sunset the evening before,—adding, that it was gorgeous, and that the grass and trees were of a beautiful Paris green!"

And again the young friends gave way to their mirth.

"One thing, dear Alice, you must consent to do for me. You must write to Miss Martha Amelia, the author of all these epistles, and tell her very plainly how indelicate her conduct is, and how utterly useless all such proceedings will prove in effecting her purpose."

"I will write this very day. You shall be no longer persecuted."

"And now let me give you a few extracts from these wonderful epistles."

So saying, Cecilia drew forth a small package of three-cornered billets, tied with a bit of pink ribbon. Taking one of them at random, she was on the point of beginning, but paused, as if her attention had been attracted by something out of doors. The sound of passing footsteps was heard on the gravel walk.

"There goes Mr. Kavanagh," said she, in a half-whisper.

Alice rose suddenly from her low chair at Cecilia's side, and the young friends looked from the window to see the clergyman pass.

"How handsome he is!" said Alice, involuntarily.

"He is, indeed."

At that moment Alice started back from the window. Kavanagh had looked up in passing, as if his eye had been drawn by some secret magnetism. A bright color flushed the cheek of Alice; her eyes fell; but Cecilia continued to look steadily into the street. Kavanagh passed on, and in a few moments was out of sight.

The two friends stood silent, side by side.

XVIII

ARTHUR KAVANAGH was descended from an ancient Catholic family. His ancestors had purchased from the Baron Victor of St. Castine a portion of his vast estates, lying upon that wild and wonderful seacoast of Maine, which, even upon the map, attracts the eye by its singular and picturesque indentations, and fills the heart of the beholder with something of that delight which throbbed in the veins of Pierre du Gast, when, with a royal charter of the land from the Atlantic to the Pacific, he sailed down the coast in all the pride of one who is to be prince of such a vast domain. Here, in the bosom of the solemn forests, they continued the practice of that faith which had first been planted there by Rasle and St. Castine; and the little church where they worshipped is still standing, though now as closed and silent as the graves which surround it, and in which the dust of the Kavanaghs lies buried.

In these solitudes, in this faith, was Kavanagh born, and grew to childhood, a feeble, delicate boy, watched over by a grave and taciturn father, and a mother who looked upon him with infinite tenderness, as upon a treasure she should not long retain. She walked with him by the seaside, and spoke to him of God, and the mysterious majesty of the ocean, with its tides and tempests. She sat with him on the carpet of golden threads beneath the aromatic pines, and, as the perpetual melancholy sound ran along the rattling boughs, his soul seemed to rise and fall, with a motion and a whisper like those in the branches over him. She taught him his letters from the Lives of the Saints,—a volume full of wondrous legends, and illustrated with engravings from pictures by the old masters, which opened to him at once the world of spirits and the world of art; and both were beautiful. She explained to him the pictures; she read to him the legends,—the lives of holy men and women, full of faith and good works,—things which ever afterward remained associated together in his mind. Thus holiness of life, and self-renunciation, and devotion to duty, were early impressed upon his soul. To his quick imagination, the spiritual world became real; the holy company of the saints stood round about the solitary boy; his guardian angels led him by the hand by day, and sat by his pillow at night. At times, even, he wished to die, that he might see them and talk with them, and return no more to his weak and weary body.

Of all the legends of the mysterious book, that which most delighted and most deeply impressed him was the legend of

St. Christopher. The picture was from a painting of Paolo Farinato, representing a figure of gigantic strength and stature, leaning upon a staff, and bearing the infant Christ on his bending shoulders across the rushing river. The legend related, that St. Christopher, being of huge proportions and immense strength, wandered long about the world before his conversion, seeking for the greatest king, and willing to obey no other. After serving various masters, whom he in turn deserted, because each recognized by some word or sign another greater than himself, he heard by chance of Christ, the king of heaven and earth, and asked of a holy hermit where he might be found, and how he might serve him. The hermit told him he must fast and pray; but the giant replied that if he fasted he should lose his strength, and that he did not know how to pray. Then the hermit told him to take up his abode on the banks of a dangerous mountain torrent, where travelers were often drowned in crossing, and to rescue any that might be in peril. The giant obeyed; and tearing up a palm tree by the roots for a staff, he took his station by the river's side, and saved many lives. And the Lord looked down from heaven and said, "Behold this strong man, who knows not yet the way to worship, but has found the way to serve me!" And one night he heard the voice of a child, crying in the darkness and saying, "Christopher! come and bear me over the river!" And he went out, and found the child sitting alone on the margin of the stream; and taking him upon his shoulders, he waded into the water. Then the wind began to roar, and the waves to rise higher and higher about him, and his little burden, which at first had seemed so light, grew heavier and heavier as he advanced, and bent his huge shoulders down, and put his life in peril; so that, when he reached the shore, he said, "Who art thou, O child, that hast weighed upon me with a weight, as if I had borne the whole world upon my shoulders?" And the little child answered, "Thou hast borne the whole world upon thy shoulders, and Him who created it. I am Christ, whom thou by thy deeds of charity wouldst serve. Thou and thy service are accepted. Plant thy staff in the ground, and it shall blossom and bear fruit!" With these words, the child vanished away.

There was something in this beautiful legend that entirely captivated the heart of the boy, and a vague sense of its hidden meaning seemed at times to seize him and control him. Later in life it became more and more evident to him, and remained forever in his mind as a lovely allegory of active charity and a willingness to serve. Like the giant's staff, it blossomed and bore fruit.

But the time at length came, when his father decreed that he must be sent away to school. It was not meet that his son should be educated as a girl. He must go to the Jesuit college in Canada. Accordingly, one bright summer morning, he departed with his father, on horseback, through those majestic forests that stretch with almost unbroken shadows from the sea to the St. Lawrence, leaving behind him all the endearments of home, and a wound in his mother's heart that never ceased to ache,—a longing, unsatisfied and insatiable, for her absent Arthur, who had gone from her perhaps forever.

At college he distinguished himself by his zeal for study, by the docility, gentleness, and generosity of his nature. There he was thoroughly trained in the classics, and in the dogmas of that august faith, whose turrets gleam with such crystalline light, and whose dungeons are so deep, and dark, and terrible. The study of philosophy and theology was congenial to his mind. Indeed, he often laid aside Homer for Parmenides, and turned from the odes of Pindar and Horace to the mystic hymns of Cleanthes and Synesius.

The uniformity of college life was broken only by the annual visit home in the summer vacation; the joyous meeting, the bitter parting; the long journey to and fro through the grand, solitary, mysterious forest. To his mother these visits were even more precious than to himself; for ever more and more they added to her boundless affection the feeling of pride and confidence and satisfaction,—the joy and beauty of a youth unspotted from the world, and glowing with the enthusiasm of virtue.

At length his college days were ended. He returned home full of youth, full of joy and hope; but it was only to receive the dying blessings of his mother, who expired in peace, having seen his face once more. Then the house became empty to him. Solitary was the seashore, solitary were the woodland walks. But the spiritual world seemed nearer and more real. For affairs he had no aptitude; and he betook himself again to his philosophic and theological studies. He pondered with fond enthusiasm on the rapturous pages of Molinos and Madame Guyon; and in a spirit akin to that which wrote, he read the writings of Santa Theresa, which he found among his mother's books,—the Meditations, the Road to Perfection, and the Moradas, or Castle of the Soul. She, too, had lingered over those pages with delight, and there were many passages marked by her own hand. Among them was this, which he often repeated to himself in his lonely walks: "O, Life, Life! how canst thou sustain thyself, being absent from thy Life? In so great a solitude, in what shalt thou employ thyself? What shalt thou do, since all thy deeds are faulty and imperfect?"

In such meditations passed many weeks and months. But mingled with them, continually and ever with more distinctness, arose in his memory from the days of childhood the old tradition of Saint Christopher,—the beautiful allegory of humility and labor. He and his service had been accepted, though he would not fast, and had not learned to pray! It became more and more clear to him, that the life of man consists not in seeing visions, and in dreaming dreams, but in active charity and willing service.

Moreover, the study of ecclesiastical history awoke within him many strange and dubious thoughts. The books taught him more than their writers meant to teach. It was impossible to read of Athanasius without reading also of Arian; it was impossible to hear of Calvin without hearing of Servetus. Reason began more energetically to vindicate itself; that Reason, which is a light in darkness, not that which is "a thorn in Revelation's side." The search after truth and freedom, both intellectual and spiritual, became a passion in his soul; and he pursued it until he had left far behind him many dusky dogmas, many antique superstitions, many time-honored observances, which the lips of her alone, who first taught them to him in his childhood, had invested with solemnity and sanctity.

By slow degrees, and not by violent spiritual conflicts, he became a Protestant. He had but passed from one chapel to another in the same vast cathedral. He was still beneath the same ample roof, still heard the same divine service chanted in a different dialect of the same universal language. Out of his old faith he brought with him all he had found in it that was holy and pure and of good report. Not its bigotry, and fanaticism, and intolerance; but its zeal, its self-devotion, its heavenly aspirations, its human sympathies, its endless deeds of charity. Not till after his father's death, however, did he become a clergyman. Then his vocation was manifest to him. He no longer hesitated, but entered upon its many duties and responsibilities, its many trials and discouragements, with the zeal of Peter and the gentleness of John.

XIX

A WEEK later, and Kavanagh was installed in his little room in the church tower. A week later, and the carrier pigeon was on the wing. A week later, and Martha Amelia's anonymous epistolary eulogies of her relative had ceased forever.

Swiftly and silently the summer advanced, and the following announcement in the Fairmeadow Advertiser proclaimed the hot weather and its alleviations:—

[76]

"I have the pleasure of announcing to the Ladies and Gentlemen of Fairmeadow and its vicinity, that my Bath House is now completed, and ready for the reception of those who are disposed to regale themselves in a luxury peculiar to the once polished Greek and noble Roman.

"To the Ladies I will say, that Tuesday of each week will be appropriated to their exclusive benefit; the white flag will be the signal; and I assure the Ladies, that due respect shall be scrupulously observed, and that they shall be guarded from each vagrant foot and each licentious eye.

EDWARD DIMPLE."

Moreover, the village was enlivened by the usual traveling shows,—the waxwork figures representing Eliza Wharton and the Salem Tragedy, to which clergymen and their families were "respectfully invited, free on presenting their cards"; a stuffed shark, that had eaten the exhibitor's father in Lynn bay; the menagerie, with its loud music and its roars of rage; the circus, with its tan and tinsel,—its faded columbine and melancholy clown; and, finally, the standard drama, in which Elder Evans, like an ancient Spanish Bululú, impersonated all the principal male characters, and was particularly imposing in Iago and the Moor, having half his face lampblacked, and turning now the luminous, now the eclipsed side to the audience, as the exigencies of the dialogue demanded.

There was also a great Temperance Jubilee, with a procession, in which was conspicuous a large horse, whose shaven tail was adorned with gay ribbons, and whose rider bore a banner with the device, "Shaved in the Cause"! Moreover, the Grand Junction Railroad was opened through the town, running in one direction to the city, and in the other into unknown northern regions, stringing the white villages like pearls upon its black thread. By this, the town lost much of its rural quiet and seclusion. The inhabitants became restless and ambitious. They were in constant excitement and alarm, like children in storybooks hidden away somewhere by an ogre, who visits them regularly every day and night, and occasionally devours one of them for a meal.

Nevertheless, most of the inhabitants considered the railroad a great advantage to the village. Several ladies were heard to say that Fairmeadow had grown quite metropolitan; and Mrs. Wilmerdings, who suffered under a chronic suspension of the mental faculties, had a vague notion, probably connected with the profession of her son, that it was soon to become a seaport.

In the fields and woods, meanwhile, there were other signs and signals of the summer. The darkening foliage; the embrowning grain; the golden dragonfly haunting the blackberry bushes; the cawing crows, that looked down from the mountain on the cornfield, and waited day after day for the scarecrow to finish his work and depart; and the smoke of far-off burning woods, that pervaded the air and hung in purple haze about the summits of the mountains,—these were the avant-couriers and attendants of the hot August.

Kavanagh had now completed the first great cycle of parochial visits. He had seen the Vaughans, the Archers, the Churchills, and also the Hawkinses and the Wilmerdingses, and many more. With Mr. Churchill he had become intimate. They had many points of contact and sympathy. They walked together on leisure afternoons; they sat together through long summer evenings; they discoursed with friendly zeal on various topics of literature, religion, and morals.

Moreover, he worked assiduously at his sermons. He preached the doctrines of Christ. He preached holiness, self-denial, love; and his hearers remarked that he almost invariably took his texts from the Evangelists, as much as possible from the words of Christ, and seldom from Paul, or the Old Testament. He did not so much denounce vice, as inculcate virtue; he did not deny, but affirm; he did not lacerate the hearts of his hearers with doubt and disbelief, but consoled, and comforted, and healed them with faith.

The only danger was that he might advance too far, and leave his congregation behind him; as a piping shepherd, who, charmed with his own music, walks over the flowery mead, not perceiving that his tardy flock is lingering far behind, more intent upon cropping the thymy food around them, than upon listening to the celestial harmonies that are gradually dying away in the distance.

His words were always kindly; he brought no railing accusation against any man; he dealt in no exaggerations nor over-statements. But while he was gentle, he was firm. He did not refrain from reprobating intemperance because one of his deacons owned a distillery; nor war, because another had a contract for supplying the army with muskets; nor slavery, because one of the great men of the village slammed his pew-door, and left the church with a grand air, as much as to say, that all that sort of thing would not do, and the clergy had better confine itself to abusing the sins of the Hindoos, and let our domestic institutions alone.

In affairs ecclesiastical he had not suggested many changes. One that he had much at heart was, that the partition wall between parish and church should be quietly taken down, so that all should sit together at the Supper of the Lord. He also desired that the organist should relinquish the old and pernicious habit of preluding with triumphal marches, and running his fingers at random over the keys of his instrument, playing scraps of secular music very slowly to make them sacred, and substitute instead some of the beautiful symphonies of Pergolesi, Palestrina, and Sebastian Bach.

He held that sacred melodies were becoming to sacred themes; and did not wish, that, in his church, as in some of the French Canadian churches, the holy profession of religion should be sung to the air of "When One is Dead 'tis for A Long Time,"—the commandments, aspirations for heaven, and the necessity of thinking of one's salvation, to "The Follies of Spain," "Louisa was Sleeping in a Grove," or a grand "March of the French Cavalry."

The study in the tower was delightful. There sat the young apostle, and meditated the great design and purpose of his life, the removal of all prejudice, and uncharitableness, and persecution, and the union of all sects into one church universal. Sects themselves he would not destroy, but sectarianism; for sects were to him only as separate converging roads, leading all to the same celestial city of peace. As he sat alone, and thought of these things, he heard the great bell boom above him, and remembered the ages when in all Christendom there was but one Church; when bells were anointed, baptized, and prayed for, that, wheresoever those holy bells should sound, all deceits of Satan, all danger of whirlwinds, thunders, lightnings, and tempests, might be driven away,—that devotion might increase in every Christian when he heard them,—and that the Lord would sanctify them with his Holy Spirit, and infuse into them the heavenly dew of the Holy Ghost. He thought of the great bell Guthlac, which an abbot of Croyland gave to his monastery, and of the six others given by his successor,—so musical, that, when they all rang together, as Ingulphus affirms, there was no ringing in England equal to it. As he listened, the bell seemed to breathe upon the air such clangorous sentences as,

"Laudo Deum verum, plebem voco, congrego clerum,
Defunctos ploro, nimbum fugo, festaque honoro."

Possibly, also, at times, it interrupted his studies and meditations with other words than these. Possibly it sang into his ears, as did the bells of Varennes into the ears of Panurge,—"Marry thee, marry thee, marry, marry; if thou shouldst marry, marry, marry, thou shalt find good therein, therein, therein, so marry, marry."

From this tower of contemplation he looked down with mingled emotions of joy and sorrow on the toiling world below. The wide prospect seemed to enlarge his sympathies and his charities; and he often thought of the words of Plato: "When we consider human life, we should view as from a high tower all things terrestrial; such as herds, armies, men employed in agriculture, in marriages, divorces, births, deaths; the tumults of courts of justice; desolate lands; various barbarous nations;

feasts, wailings, markets, a medley of all things, in a system adorned by contrarieties."

On the outside of the door Kavanagh had written the vigorous line of Dante,

"Think that Today shall never dawn again!"

that it might always serve as a salutation and memento to him as he entered. On the inside, the no less striking lines of a more modern bard,—

"Lose this day loitering, 't will be the same story
Tomorrow, and the next more dilatory.
The indecision brings its own delays,
And days are lost, lamenting o'er lost days.
Are you in earnest? Seize this very minute!
What you can do or think you can, begin it!
Boldness has genius, power, and magic in it!
Only engage, and then the mind grows heated:
Begin it, and the work will be completed."

Once, as he sat in this retreat near noon, enjoying the silence, and the fresh air that visited him through the oval windows, his attention was arrested by a cloud of dust, rolling along the road, out of which soon emerged a white horse, and then a very singular, round-shouldered, old-fashioned chaise, containing an elderly couple, both in black. What particularly struck him was the gait of the horse, who had a very disdainful fling to his hind legs. The slow equipage passed, and would have been forever forgotten, had not Kavanagh seen it again at sunset, stationary at Mr. Churchill's door, towards which he was directing his steps.

As he entered, he met Mr. Churchill, just taking leave of an elderly lady and gentleman in black, whom he recognized as the travelers in the old chaise. Mr. Churchill looked a little flushed and disturbed, and bade his guests farewell with a constrained air. On seeing Kavanagh, he saluted him, and called him by name; whereupon the lady pursed up her mouth, and, after a quick glance, turned away her face; and the gentleman passed with a lofty look, in which curiosity, reproof, and pious indignation were strangely mingled. They got into the chaise, with some such feelings as Noah and his wife may be supposed to have had on entering the ark; the whip descended upon the old horse with unusual vigor, accompanied by a jerk of the reins that caused him to say within himself, "What is the matter now?" He then moved off at his usual pace, and with that peculiar motion of the hind legs which Kavanagh had perceived in the morning.

Kavanagh found his friend not a little disturbed, and evidently by the conversation of the departed guests.

"That old gentleman," said Mr. Churchill, "is your predecessor, Mr. Pendexter. He thinks we are in a bad way since he left us. He considers your liberality as nothing better than rank Arianism and infidelity. The fact is, the old gentleman is a little soured; the vinous fermentation in his veins is now over, and the acetous has commenced."

Kavanagh smiled, but made no answer.

"I, of course, defended you stoutly," continued Mr. Churchill; "but if he goes about the village sowing such seed, there will be tares growing with the wheat."

"I have no fears," said Kavanagh, very quietly.

Mr. Churchill's apprehensions were not, however, groundless; for in the course of the week it came out that doubts, surmises, and suspicions of Kavanagh's orthodoxy were springing up in many weak but worthy minds. And it was ever after observed, that, whenever that fatal, apocalyptic white horse and antediluvian chaise appeared in town, many parishioners were harassed with doubts and perplexed with theological difficulties and uncertainties.

Nevertheless, the main current of opinion was with him; and the parish showed their grateful acknowledgment of his zeal and sympathy, by requesting him to sit for his portrait to a great artist from the city, who was passing the summer months in the village for recreation, using his pencil only on rarest occasions and as a particular favor. To this martyrdom the

meek Kavanagh submitted without a murmur. During the progress of this work of art, he was seldom left alone; some one
of his parishioners was there to enliven him; and most frequently
it was Miss Martha Amelia Hawkins, who had become very
devout of late, being zealous in the Sunday School, and requesting her relative not to walk between churches any more. She
took a very lively interest in the portrait, and favored with
many suggestions the distinguished artist, who found it difficult
to obtain an expression which would satisfy the parish, some
wishing to have it grave, if not severe, and others with "Mr.
Kavanagh's peculiar smile." Kavanagh himself was quite indif-
ferent about the matter, and met his fate with Christian fortitude,
in a white cravat and sacerdotal robes, with one hand hanging
down from the back of his chair, and the other holding a large
book with the forefinger between its leaves, reminding Mr.
Churchill of Milo with his fingers in the oak. The expression of
the face was exceedingly bland and resigned; perhaps a little
wanting in strength, but on the whole satisfactory to the parish.
So was the artist's price; nay, it was even held by some persons
to be cheap, considering the quantity of background he had
put in.

XX

MEANWHILE, things had gone on very quietly and monoto-
nously in Mr. Churchill's family. Only one event, and that a
mysterious one, had disturbed its serenity. It was the sudden
disappearance of Lucy, the pretty orphan girl; and as the
booted centipede, who had so much excited Mr. Churchill's
curiosity, disappeared at the same time, there was little doubt
that they had gone away together. But whither gone, and wherefore, remained a mystery.

Mr. Churchill, also, had had his profile, and those of his wife and children, taken, in a very humble style, by Mr. Bantam, whose advertisement he had noticed on his way to school nearly a year before. His own was considered the best, as a work of art. The face was cut out entirely; the collar of the coat velvet; the shirt collar very high and white; and the top of his head ornamented with a crest of hair turning up in front, though his own turned down,—which slight deviation from nature was explained and justified by the painter as a license allowable in art.

One evening, as he was sitting down to begin for at least the hundredth time the great Romance,—subject of so many resolves and so much remorse, so often determined upon but never begun,—a loud knock at the street door, which stood wide open, announced a visitor. Unluckily, the study door was likewise open; and consequently, being in full view, he found it impossible to refuse himself; nor, in fact, would he have done so, had all the doors been shut and bolted,—the art of refusing one's self being at that time but imperfectly understood in Fairmeadow. Accordingly, the visitor was shown in.

He announced himself as Mr. Hathaway. Passing through the village, he could not deny himself the pleasure of calling on Mr. Churchill, whom he knew by his writings in the periodicals, though not personally. He wished, moreover, to secure the coöperation of one already so favorably known to the literary world, in a new Magazine he was about to establish, in order to raise the character of American literature, which, in his opinion, the existing reviews and magazines had entirely failed to accomplish. A daily increasing want of something better was felt by the public; and the time had come for the establishment of such a periodical as he proposed. After explaining in rather a florid and exuberant manner his plan and prospects, he entered more at large into the subject of American literature, which it was his design to foster and patronize.

"I think, Mr. Churchill," said he, "that we want a national literature commensurate with our mountains and rivers,—commensurate with Niagara, and the Alleghenies, and the Great Lakes!"

"Oh!"

"We want a national epic that shall correspond to the size of the country; that shall be to all other epics what Banvard's Panorama of the Mississippi is to all other paintings,—the largest in the world!"

"Ah!"

"We want a national drama in which scope enough shall be given to our gigantic ideas, and to the unparalleled activity and progress of our people!"

"Of course."

"In a word, we want a national literature altogether shaggy and unshorn, that shall shake the earth, like a herd of buffaloes thundering over the prairies!"

"Precisely," interrupted Mr. Churchill; "but excuse me!—are you not confounding things that have no analogy? Great has a very different meaning when applied to a river, and when applied to a literature. Large and shallow may perhaps be applied to both. Literature is rather an image of the spiritual world, than of the physical, is it not?—of the internal, rather than the external. Mountains, lakes, and rivers are, after all, only its scenery and decorations, not its substance and essence. A man will not necessarily be a great poet because he lives near a great mountain. Nor, being a poet, will he necessarily write better poems than another, because he lives nearer Niagara."

"But, Mr. Churchill, you do not certainly mean to deny the influence of scenery on the mind?"

"No, only to deny that it can create genius. At best, it can only develop it. Switzerland has produced no extraordinary poet; nor, as far as I know, have the Andes, or the Himalaya mountains, or the Mountains of the Moon in Africa."

"But, at all events," urged Mr. Hathaway, "let us have our literature national. If it is not national, it is nothing."

"On the contrary, it may be a great deal. Nationality is a

good thing to a certain extent, but universality is better. All that is best in the great poets of all countries is not what is national in them, but what is universal. Their roots are in their native soil; but their branches wave in the unpatriotic air, that speaks the same language unto all men, and their leaves shine with the illimitable light that pervades all lands. Let us throw all the windows open; let us admit the light and air on all sides; that we may look towards the four corners of the heavens, and not always in the same direction."

"But you admit nationality to be a good thing?"

"Yes, if not carried too far; still, I confess, it rather limits one's views of truth. I prefer what is natural. Mere nationality is often ridiculous. Every one smiles when he hears the Icelandic proverb, 'Iceland is the best land the sun shines upon.' Let us be natural, and we shall be national enough. Besides, our literature can be strictly national only so far as our character and modes of thought differ from those of other nations. Now, as we are very like the English,—are, in fact, English under a different sky,—I do not see how our literature can be very different from theirs. Westward from hand to hand we pass the lighted torch, but it was lighted at the old domestic fireside of England."

"Then you think our literature is never to be any thing but an imitation of the English?"

"Not at all. It is not an imitation, but, as some one has said, a continuation."

"It seems to me that you take a very narrow view of the subject."

"On the contrary, a very broad one. No literature is complete until the language in which it is written is dead. We may well be proud of our task and of our position. Let us see if we can build in any way worthy of our forefathers."

"But I insist upon originality."

"Yes; but without spasms and convulsions. Authors must not, like Chinese soldiers, expect to win victories by turning somersets in the air."

"Well, really, the prospect from your point of view is not very brilliant. Pray, what do you think of our national literature?"

"Simply, that a national literature is not the growth of a day. Centuries must contribute their dew and sunshine to it. Our own is growing slowly but surely, striking its roots downward, and its branches upward, as is natural; and I do not wish, for the sake of what some people call originality, to invert it, and try to make it grow with its roots in the air. And as for having it so savage and wild as you want it, I have only to say, that all literature, as well as all art, is the result of culture and intellectual refinement."

"Ah! we do not want art and refinement; we want genius,— untutored, wild, original, free."

"But, if this genius is to find any expression, it must employ art; for art is the external expression of our thoughts. Many have genius, but, wanting art, are forever dumb. The two must go together to form the great poet, painter, or sculptor."

"In that sense, very well."

"I was about to say also that I thought our literature would finally not be wanting in a kind of universality.

"As the blood of all nations is mingling with our own, so will their thoughts and feelings finally mingle in our literature. We shall draw from the Germans tenderness; from the Spaniards, passion; from the French, vivacity, to mingle more and more with our English solid sense. And this will give us universality, so much to be desired."

"If that is your way of thinking," interrupted the visitor, "you will like the work I am now engaged upon."

"What is it?"

"A great national drama, the scene of which is laid in New Mexico. It is entitled Don Serafin, or the Marquis of the Seven Churches. The principal characters are Don Serafin, an old Spanish hidalgo; his daughter Deseada; and Fra Serapion, the curate. The play opens with Fra Serapion at breakfast; on the table a gamecock, tied by the leg, sharing his master's meal. Then follows a scene at the cockpit, where the Marquis stakes the remnant of his fortune—his herds and hacienda—on a favorite cock, and loses."

"But what do you know about cockfighting?" demanded, rather than asked, the astonished and half-laughing schoolmaster.

"I am not very well informed on that subject, and I was going to ask you if you could not recommend some work."

"The only work I am acquainted with," replied Mr. Churchill, "is the Reverend Mr. Pegge's Essay on Cockfighting among the Ancients; and I hardly see how you could apply that to the Mexicans."

"Why, they are a kind of ancients, you know. I certainly will hunt up the essay you mention, and see what I can do with it."

"And all I know about the matter itself," continued Mr. Churchill, "is, that Mark Antony was a patron of the pit, and that his cocks were always beaten by Cæsar's; and that, when Themistocles the Athenian general was marching against the Persians, he halted his army to see a cockfight, and made a speech to his soldiery, to the effect, that those animals fought not for the gods of their country, nor for the monuments of their ancestors, nor for glory, nor for freedom, nor for their children, but only for the sake of victory. On his return to Athens, he established cockfights in that capital. But how this is to help you in Mexico I do not see, unless you introduce Santa Anna, and compare him to Cæsar and Themistocles."

"That is it; I will do so. It will give historic interest to the play. I thank you for the suggestion."

"The subject is certainly very original; but it does not strike me as particularly national."

"Prospective, you see!" said Mr. Hathaway, with a penetrating look.

"Ah, yes; I perceive you fish with a heavy sinker,—down, far down in the future,—among posterity, as it were."

"You have seized the idea. Besides, I obviate your objection, by introducing an American circus company from the United

States, which enables me to bring horses on the stage and produce great scenic effect."

"That is a bold design. The critics will be out upon you without fail."

"Never fear that. I know the critics root and branch,—out and out,—have summered them and wintered them,—in fact, am one of them myself. Very good fellows are the critics; are they not?"

"O, yes; only they have such a pleasant way of talking down upon authors."

"If they did not talk down upon them, they would show no superiority; and, of course, that would never do."

"Nor is it to be wondered at, that authors are sometimes a little irritable. I often recall the poet in the Spanish fable, whose manuscripts were devoured by mice, till at length he put some corrosive sublimate into his ink, and was never troubled again."

"Why don't you try it yourself?" said Mr. Hathaway, rather sharply.

"O," answered Mr. Churchill, with a smile of humility, "I and my writings are too insignificant. They may gnaw and welcome. I do not like to have poison about, even for such purposes."

"By the way, Mr. Churchill," said the visitor, adroitly changing the subject, "do you know Honeywell?"

"No, I do not. Who is he?"

"Honeywell the poet, I mean."

"No, I never even heard of him. There are so many poets nowadays!"

"That is very strange indeed! Why, I consider Honeywell one of the finest writers in the country,—quite in the front rank of American authors. He is a real poet, and no mistake. Nature made him with her shirtsleeves rolled up."

"What has he published?"

"He has not published anything yet, except in the newspapers. But, this autumn, he is going to bring out a volume of poems. I could not help having my joke with him about it. I told him he had better print it on cartridge paper."

"Why so?"

"Why, to make it go off better; don't you understand?"

"O, yes; now that you explain it. Very good."

"Honeywell is going to write for the Magazine; he is to furnish a poem for every number; and as he succeeds equally well in the plaintive and didactic style of Wordsworth, and the more vehement and impassioned style of Byron, I think we shall do very well."

"And what do you mean to call the new Magazine?" inquired Mr. Churchill.

"We think of calling it The Niagara."

"Why, that is the name of our fire engine! Why not call it The Extinguisher?"

"That is also a good name; but I prefer The Niagara, as more national. And I hope, Mr. Churchill, you will let us count upon you. We should like to have an article from your pen for every number."

"Do you mean to pay your contributors?"

"Not the first year, I am sorry to say. But after that, if the work succeeds, we shall pay handsomely. And, of course, it will succeed, for we mean it shall; and we never say fail. There is no such word in our dictionary. Before the year is out, we mean to print fifty thousand copies; and fifty thousand copies will give us, at least, one hundred and fifty thousand readers; and, with such an audience, any author might be satisfied."

He had touched at length the right strings in Mr. Churchill's bosom; and they vibrated to the touch with pleasant harmonies. Literary vanity!—literary ambition! The editor perceived it; and so cunningly did he play upon these chords, that, before he departed, Mr. Churchill had promised to write for him a series of papers on Obscure Martyrs,—a kind of tragic history of the unrecorded and lifelong sufferings of women, which hitherto had found no historian, save now and then a novelist.

Notwithstanding the certainty of success,—notwithstanding the fifty thousand subscribers and the one hundred and fifty thousand readers,—the Magazine never went into operation. Still the dream was enough to occupy Mr. Churchill's thoughts, and to withdraw them entirely from his Romance for many weeks together.

XXI

EVERY state, and almost every county, of New England, has its roaring brook,—a mountain streamlet, overhung by woods, impeded by a mill, encumbered by fallen trees, but ever racing, rushing, roaring down through gurgling gullies, and filling the forest with its delicious sound and freshness; the drinking place of home-returning herds; the mysterious haunt of squirrels and blue jays; the sylvan retreat of schoolgirls, who frequent it on summer holidays, and mingle their restless thoughts, their over-flowing fancies, their fair imaginings, with its restless, exuberant, and rejoicing stream.

Fairmeadow had no roaring brook. As its name indicates, it was too level a land for that. But the neighboring town of West-wood, lying more inland, and among the hills, had one of the fairest and fullest of all the brooks that roar. It was the boast of the neighborhood. Not to have seen it, was to have seen no brook, no waterfall, no mountain ravine. And, consequently, to behold it and admire, was Kavanagh taken by Mr. Churchill as soon as the summer vacation gave leisure and opportunity. The party consisted of Mr. and Mrs. Churchill, and Alfred, in a one-horse chaise; and Cecilia, Alice, and Kavanagh, in a carryall,—the fourth seat in which was occupied by a large basket, containing what the Squire of the Grove, in Don Quixote, called his "fiambreras,"—that magniloquent Castilian word for cold collation. Over warm uplands, smelling of clover and mint; through cool glades, still wet with the rain of yesterday; along the river; across the rattling and tilting planks of wooden bridges; by orchards; by the gates of fields, with the tall mullen growing at the bars; by stone walls overrun with privet and barberries; in sun and heat, in shadow and coolness, —forward drove the happy party on that pleasant summer morning.

At length they reached the roaring brook. From a gorge in the mountains, through a long, winding gallery of birch, and beech, and pine, leaped the bright, brown waters of the jubilant streamlet; out of the woods, across the plain, under the rude bridge of logs, into the woods again,—a day between two nights. With it went a song that made the heart sing likewise; a song of joy, and exultation, and freedom; a continuous and unbroken song of life, and pleasure, and perpetual youth. Like the old Icelandic Scald, the streamlet seemed to say,—

"I am possessed of songs such as neither the spouse of a king, nor any son of man, can repeat: one of them is called the Helper; it will help thee at thy need, in sickness, grief, and all adversity."

The little party left their carriages at a farmhouse by the bridge, and followed the rough road on foot along the brook; now close upon it, now shut out by intervening trees. Mr. Churchill, bearing the basket on his arm, walked in front with his wife and Alfred. Kavanagh came behind with Cecilia and Alice. The music of the brook silenced all conversation; only occasional exclamations of delight were uttered,—the irrepressible applause of fresh and sensitive natures, in a scene so lovely. Presently, turning off from the road, which led directly to the mill, and was rough with the tracks of heavy wheels, they went down to the margin of the brook.

"How indescribably beautiful this brown water is!" exclaimed Kavanagh. "It is like wine, or the nectar of the gods of Olympus; as if the falling Hebe had poured it from the goblet."

"More like the mead or metheglin of the northern gods," said Mr. Churchill, "spilled from the drinking-horns of Valhalla."

But all the ladies thought Kavanagh's comparison the better of the two, and in fact the best that could be made; and Mr. Churchill was obliged to retract and apologize for his allusion to the celestial alehouse of Odin.

Ere long they were forced to cross the brook, stepping from stone to stone, over the little rapids and cascades. All crossed lightly, easily, safely; even "the sumpter mule," as Mr. Churchill called himself, on account of the pannier. Only Cecilia lingered behind, as if afraid to cross. Cecilia, who had crossed at that same place a hundred times before,—Cecilia, who had the surest foot, and the firmest nerves, of all the village maidens,— she now stood irresolute, seized with a sudden tremor; blushing, and laughing at her own timidity, and yet unable to advance. Kavanagh saw her embarrassment, and hastened back to help her. Her hand trembled in his; she thanked him with a gentle look and word. His whole soul was softened within him. His attitude, his countenance, his voice, were alike submissive and subdued. He was as one penetrated with tenderest emotions.

It is difficult to know at what moment love begins; it is less difficult to know that it has begun. A thousand heralds proclaim it to the listening air; a thousand ministers and messengers betray it to the eye. Tone, act, attitude and look,—the signals upon the countenance,—the electric telegraph of touch;—all these betray the yielding citadel before the word itself is uttered, which, like the key surrendered, opens every avenue and gate of entrance, and makes retreat impossible!

The day passed delightfully with all. They sat upon the stones and the roots of trees. Cecilia read, from a volume she had brought with her, poems that rhymed with the running water. The others listened and commented. Little Alfred waded in the stream, with his bare white feet, and launched boats over the falls. Noon had been fixed upon for dining; but they antici- pated it by at least an hour. The great basket was opened;

endless sandwiches were drawn forth, and a cold pastry, as large as that of the Squire of the Grove. During the repast, Mr. Churchill slipped into the brook, while in the act of handing a sandwich to his wife, which caused unbounded mirth; and Kavanagh sat down on a mossy trunk, that gave way beneath him, and crumbled into powder. This, also, was received with great merriment.

After dinner, they ascended the brook still farther,—indeed, quite to the mill, which was not going. It had been stopped in the midst of its work. The saw still held its hungry teeth fixed in the heart of a pine. Mr. Churchill took occasion to make known to the company his long cherished purpose of writing a poem called "The Song of the Saw-Mill," and enlarged on the beautiful associations of flood and forest connected with the theme. He delighted himself and his audience with the fine fancies he meant to weave into his poem, and wondered nobody had thought of the subject before. Kavanagh said it had been thought of before; and cited Kerner's little poem, so charmingly translated by Bryant. Mr. Churchill had not seen it. Kavanagh looked into his pocketbook for it, but it was not to be found; still he was sure that there was such a poem. Mr. Churchill abandoned his design. He had spoken,—and the treasure, just as he touched it with his hand, was gone forever.

The party returned home as it came, all tired and happy, excepting little Alfred, who was tired and cross, and sat sleepy and sagging on his father's knee, with his hat cocked rather fiercely over his eyes.

XXII

THE brown autumn came. Out of doors, it brought to the fields the prodigality of the yellow harvest,—to the forest, revelations of light,—and to the sky, the sharp air, the morning mist, the red clouds at evening. Within doors, the sense of seclusion, the stillness of closed and curtained windows, musings by the fireside, books, friends, conversation, and the long, meditative evenings. To the farmer, it brought surcease of toil,—to the scholar, that sweet delirium of the brain which changes toil to pleasure. It brought the wild duck back to the reedy marshes of the south; it brought the wild song back to the fervid brain of the poet. Without, the village street was paved with gold; the river ran red with the reflection of the leaves. Within, the faces of friends brightened the gloomy walls; the returning footsteps of the long absent gladdened the threshold; and all the sweet amenities of social life again resumed their interrupted reign.

Kavanagh preached a sermon on the coming of autumn. He chose his text from Isaiah,—"Who is this that cometh from Edom, with dyed garments from Bozrah? this that is glorious in his apparel, traveling in the greatness of his strength? Wherefore art thou red in thine apparel, and thy garments like him that treadeth in the wine vat?"

To Mr. Churchill, this beloved season—this Joseph with his coat of many colors, as he was fond of calling it—brought an unexpected guest, the forlorn, forsaken Lucy. The surmises of the family were too true. She had wandered away with the Briareus of boots. She returned alone, in destitution and despair; and often, in the grief of a broken heart and a bewildered brain, was heard to say,—

"O, how I wish I were a Christian! If I were only a Christian, I would not live any longer; I would kill myself! I am too wretched!"

A few days afterwards, a gloomy-looking man rode through the town on horseback, stopping at every corner, and crying into every street, with a loud and solemn voice,—

"Prepare! prepare! prepare to meet the living God!"

It was one of that fanatical sect, who believed the end of the world was imminent, and had prepared their ascension robes to be lifted up in clouds of glory, while the worn-out, weary world was to burn with fire beneath them, and a new and fairer earth to be prepared for their inheritance. The appearance of this forerunner of the end of the world was followed by numerous camp meetings, held in the woods near the village, to whose white tents and leafy chapels many went for consolation and found despair.

XXIII

AGAIN the two crumbly old women sat and talked together in the little parlor of the gloomy house under the poplars, and the two girls sat above, holding each other by the hand, thoughtful, and speaking only at intervals.

Alice was unusually sad and silent. The mists were already gathering over her vision,—those mists that were to deepen and darken as the season advanced, until the external world should be shrouded and finally shut from her view. Already the landscape began to wear a pale and sickly hue, as if the sun were withdrawing farther and farther, and were soon wholly to disappear, as in a northern winter. But to brighten this northern winter there now arose within her a soft, auroral light. Yes, the auroral light of love, blushing through the whole heaven of her thoughts. She had not breathed that word to herself, nor did she recognize any thrill of passion in the new emotion she experienced. But love it was; and it lifted her soul into a region, which she at once felt was native to it,— into a subtler ether, which seemed its natural element.

This feeling, however, was not all exhilaration. It brought with it its own peculiar languor and sadness, its fluctuations and swift vicissitudes of excitement and depression. To this the trivial circumstances of life contributed. Kavanagh had met her in the street, and had passed her without recognition; and, in the bitterness of the moment, she forgot that she wore a thick veil, which entirely concealed her face. At an evening party at Mr. Churchill's, by a kind of fatality, Kavanagh had stood very near her for a long time, but with his back turned, conversing with Miss Hawkins, from whose toils he was, in fact, though vainly, struggling to extricate himself; and, in the irritation of supposed neglect, Alice, had said to herself,—

"This is the kind of woman which most fascinates men!"

But these cruel moments of pain were few and short, while those of delight were many and lasting. In a life so lonely, and with so little to enliven and embellish it as hers, the guest in disguise was welcomed with ardor, and entertained without fear or suspicion. Had he been feared or suspected, he would have been no longer dangerous. He came as friendship, where friendship was most needed; he came as devotion, where her holy ministrations were always welcome.

Somewhat differently had the same passion come to the heart of Cecilia; for as the heart is, so is love to the heart. It partakes of its strength or weakness, its health or disease. In Cecilia, it but heightened the keen sensation of life. To all eyes, she became more beautiful, more radiant, more lovely, though they knew not why. When she and Kavanagh first met, it was hardly as strangers meet, but rather as friends long separated. When they first spoke to each other, it seemed but as the renewal of some previous interrupted conversation. Their souls flowed together at once, without turbulence or agitation, like waters on the same level. As they found each other without seeking, so their intercourse was without affectation and without embarrassment.

Thus, while Alice, unconsciously to herself, desired the love of Kavanagh, Cecilia, as unconsciously, assumed it as already her own. Alice keenly felt her own unworthiness; Cecilia made no comparison of merit. When Kavanagh was present, Alice was happy, but embarrassed; Cecilia, joyous and natural. The former feared she might displease; the latter divined from the first that she already pleased. In both, this was the intuition of the heart.

So sat the friends together, as they had done so many times before. But now, for the first time, each cherished a secret, which she did not confide to the other. Daily, for many weeks, the feathered courier had come and gone from window to window, but this secret had never been entrusted to his keeping. Almost daily the friends had met and talked together, but this secret had not been told. That could not be confided to another, which had not been confided to themselves; that could not be fashioned into words, which was not yet fashioned into thoughts, but was still floating, vague and formless, through the mind. Nay, had it been stated in words, each, perhaps, would have denied it. The distinct apparition of this fair spirit, in a visible form, would have startled them; though, while it haunted all the chambers of their souls as an invisible presence, it gave them only solace and delight.

"How very feverish your hand is, dearest!" said Cecilia. "What is the matter? Are you unwell?"

"Those are the very words my mother said to me this morning," replied Alice. "I feel rather languid and tired, that is all. I could not sleep last night; I never can, when it rains."

"Did it rain last night? I did not hear it."

"Yes; about midnight, quite hard. I listened to it for hours. I love to lie awake, and hear the drops fall on the roof, and on the leaves. It throws me into a delicious, dreamy state, which I like much better than sleep."

Cecilia looked tenderly at her pale face. Her eyes were very bright, and on each cheek was a crimson signal, the sight of which would have given her mother so much anguish, that, perhaps, it was better for her to be blind than to see.

"When you enter the land of dreams, Alice, you come into my peculiar realm. I am the queen of that country, you know. But, of late, I have thought of resigning my throne. These endless reveries are really a great waste of time and strength."

"Do you think so?"

"Yes; and Mr. Kavanagh thinks so, too. We talked about it the other evening; and afterwards, upon reflection, I thought he was right."

And the friends resolved, half in jest and half in earnest, that, from that day forth, the gate of their daydreams should be closed. And closed it was, ere long;—for one, by the Angel of Life; for the other, by the Angel of Death!

XXIV

THE project of the new Magazine being heard of no more, and Mr. Churchill being consequently deprived of his one hundred and fifty thousand readers, he laid aside the few notes he had made for his papers on the Obscure Martyrs, and turned his thoughts again to the great Romance. A whole leisure Saturday afternoon was before him,—pure gold, without alloy. Ere beginning his task, he stepped forth into his garden to inhale the sunny air, and let his thoughts recede a little, in order to leap farther. When he returned, glowing and radiant with poetic fancies, he found, to his unspeakable dismay, an unknown damsel sitting in his armchair. She was rather gayly yet elegantly dressed, and wore a veil, which she raised as Mr. Churchill entered, fixing upon him the full, liquid orbs of her large eyes.

"Mr. Churchill, I suppose?" said she, rising, and stepping forward.

"The same," replied the schoolmaster, with dignified courtesy.

"And will you permit me," she continued, not without a certain serene self-possession, "to introduce myself, for want of a better person to do it for me? My name is Cartwright,—Clarissa Cartwright."

This announcement did not produce that powerful and instantaneous effect on Mr. Churchill which the speaker seemed to anticipate, or at least to hope. His eye did not brighten with any quick recognition, nor did he suddenly exclaim,—

"What! Are you Miss Cartwright, the poetess, whose delightful effusions I have seen in all the magazines?"

On the contrary, he looked rather blank and expectant, and only said,—

"I am very glad to see you; pray sit down."

So that the young lady herself was obliged to communicate the literary intelligence above alluded to, which she did very gracefully, and then added,—

"I have come to ask a great favor of you, Mr. Churchill, which I hope you will not deny me. By the advice of some friends, I have collected my poems together,"—and here she drew forth from a paper a large, thin manuscript, bound in crimson velvet,—"and think of publishing them in a volume. Now, would you not do me the favor to look them over, and give me your candid opinion, whether they are worth publishing? I should value your advice so highly!"

This simultaneous appeal to his vanity and his gallantry from a fair young girl, standing on the verge of that broad, dangerous ocean, in which so many have perished, and looking wistfully over its flashing waters to the shores of the green Isle of Palms,—such an appeal, from such a person, it was impossible for Mr. Churchill to resist. He made, however, a faint show of resistance,—a feeble grasping after some excuse for refusal,—and then yielded. He received from Clarissa's delicate, trembling hand the precious volume, and from her eyes a still more precious look of thanks, and then said,—

"What name do you propose to give the volume?"

"Symphonies of the Soul, and other Poems," said the young lady; "and, if you like them, and it would not be asking too much, I should be delighted to have you write a Preface, to introduce the work to the public. The publisher says it would increase the sale very considerably."

"Ah, the publisher! yes, but that is not very complimentary to yourself," suggested Mr. Churchill. "I can already see your Poems rebelling against the intrusion of my Preface, and rising like so many nuns in a convent to expel the audacious foot that has dared to invade their sacred precincts."

But it was all in vain, this pale effort at pleasantry. Objection was useless; and the softhearted schoolmaster a second time yielded gracefully to his fate, and promised the Preface. The young lady took her leave with a profusion of thanks and blushes; and the dainty manuscript, with its delicate chirography and crimson cover, remained in the hands of Mr. Churchill, who gazed at it less as a Paradise of Dainty Devices than as a deed or mortgage of so many precious hours of his own scanty inheritance of time.

Afterwards, when he complained a little of this to his wife,—who, during the interview, had peeped in at the door, and, seeing how he was occupied, had immediately withdrawn,—she said that nobody was to blame but himself; that he should learn to say "No!" and not do just as every romantic little girl from the Academy wanted him to do; adding, as a final aggravation and climax of reproof, that she really believed he never would, and never meant to, begin his Romance!

XXV

Not long afterwards, Kavanagh and Mr. Churchill took a stroll together across the fields, and down green lanes, walking all the bright, brief afternoon. From the summit of the hill, beside the old windmill, they saw the sun set; and, opposite, the full moon rise, dewy, large, and red. As they descended, they felt the heavy dampness of the air, like water, rising to meet them,—bathing with coolness first their feet, then their hands, then their faces, till they were submerged in that sea of dew. As they skirted the woodland on their homeward way, trampling the golden leaves under foot, they heard voices at a distance, singing; and then saw the lights of the camp meeting gleaming through the trees, and, drawing nearer, distinguished a portion of the hymn:—

> "Don't you hear the Lord a-coming
> To the old churchyards,
> With a band of music,
> With a band of music,
> With a band of music,
> Sounding through the air?"

These words, at once awful and ludicrous, rose on the still twilight air from a hundred voices, thrilling with emotion, and from as many beating, fluttering, struggling hearts. High above them all was heard one voice, clear and musical as a clarion.

"I know that voice," said Mr. Churchill; "it is Elder Evans's."

"Ah!" exclaimed Kavanagh,—for only the impression of awe was upon him,—"he never acted in a deeper tragedy than this! How terrible it is! Let us pass on."

They hurried away, Kavanagh trembling in every fibre. Silently they walked, the music fading into softest vibrations behind them.

"How strange is this fanaticism!" at length said Mr. Churchill, rather as a relief to his own thoughts, than for the purpose of reviving the conversation. "These people really believe that the end of the world is close at hand."

"And to thousands," answered Kavanagh, "this is no fiction,— no illusion of an overheated imagination. Today, tomorrow, every day, to thousands, the end of the world is close at hand. And why should we fear it? We walk here as it were in the crypts of life; at times, from the great cathedral above us, we can hear the organ and the chanting of the choir; we see the light stream through the open door, when some friend goes up before us; and shall we fear to mount the narrow staircase of the grave, that leads us out of this uncertain twilight into the serene mansions of the life eternal?"

They reached the wooden bridge over the river, which the moonlight converted into a river of light. Their footsteps sounded on the planks; they passed without perceiving a female figure that stood in the shadow below on the brink of the stream, watching wistfully the steady flow of the current. It was Lucy! Her bonnet and shawl were lying at her feet; and when they had passed, she waded far out into the shallow stream, laid herself gently down in its deeper waves, and floated slowly away into the moonlight, among the golden leaves that were faded and fallen like herself,—among the water lilies, whose fragant white blossoms had been broken off and polluted long ago. Without a struggle, without a sigh, without a sound, she floated downward, downward, and silently sank into the silent river. Far off, faint, and indistinct, was heard the startling hymn, with its wild and peculiar melody,—

"O, there will be mourning, mourning, mourning, mourning,—
O, there will be mourning at the judgment-seat of Christ!"

Kavanagh's heart was full of sadness. He left Mr. Churchill at his door, and proceeded homeward. On passing his church, he could not resist the temptation to go in. He climbed to his chamber in the tower, lighted by the moon. He sat for a long time gazing from the window, and watching a distant and feeble candle, whose rays scarcely reached him across the brilliant moonlighted air. Gentler thoughts stole over him; an invisible presence soothed him; an invisible hand was laid upon his head, and the trouble and unrest of his spirit were changed to peace.

"Answer me, thou mysterious future!" exclaimed he; "tell me, —shall these things be according to my desire?"

And the mysterious future, interpreted by those desires, replied,—

"Soon thou shalt know all. It shall be well with thee!"

XXVI

On the following morning, Kavanagh sat as usual in his study in the tower. No traces were left of the heaviness and sadness of the preceding night. It was a bright, warm morning; and the window, open towards the south, let in the genial sunshine. The odor of decaying leaves scented the air; far off flashed the hazy river.

Kavanagh's heart, however, was not at rest. At times he rose from his books, and paced up and down his little study; then took up his hat as if to go out; then laid it down again, and again resumed his books. At length he arose, and, leaning on the window sill, gazed for a long time on the scene before him. Some thought was laboring in his bosom, some doubt or fear, which alternated with hope, but thwarted any fixed resolve.

Ah, how pleasantly that fair autumnal landscape smiled upon him! The great golden elms that marked the line of the village street, and under whose shadows no beggars sat; the air of comfort and plenty, of neatness, thrift, and equality, visible everywhere; and from far-off farms the sound of flails, beating the triumphal march of Ceres through the land;—these were the sights and sounds that greeted him as he looked. Silently the yellow leaves fell upon the graves in the churchyard; and the dew glistened in the grass, which was still long and green.

Presently his attention was arrested by a dove, pursued by a little kingfisher, who constantly endeavored to soar above it, in order to attack it at greater advantage. The flight of the birds, thus shooting through the air at arrowy speed, was beautiful. When they were opposite the tower, the dove suddenly wheeled, and darted in at the open window, while the pursuer held on his way with a long sweep, and was out of sight in a moment.

At the first glance, Kavanagh recognized the dove, which lay panting on the floor. It was the same he had seen Cecilia buy of the little man in gray. He took it in his hands. Its heart was beating violently. About its neck was a silken band; beneath its wing, a billet, upon which was a single word, "Cecilia." The bird, then, was on its way to Cecilia Vaughan. He hailed the omen as auspicious, and, immediately closing the window, seated himself at his table, and wrote a few hurried words, which, being carefully folded and sealed, he fastened to the band, and then hastily, as if afraid his purpose might be changed by delay, opened the window and set the bird at liberty. It sailed once or twice round the tower, apparently uncertain and bewildered, or still in fear of its pursuer. Then, instead of holding its way over the fields to Cecilia Vaughan, it darted over the roofs of the village, and alighted at the window of Alice Archer.

Having written that morning to Cecilia something urgent and confidential, she was already waiting the answer; and, not doubting that the bird had brought it, she hastily untied the silken band, and, without looking at the superscription, opened the first note that fell on the table. It was very brief; only a few lines, and not a name mentioned in it; an impulse, an ejaculation of love; every line quivering with electric fire,—

every word a pulsation of the writer's heart. It was signed "Arthur Kavanagh."

Overwhelmed by the suddenness and violence of her emotions, Alice sat for a long time motionless, holding the open letter in her hand. Then she read it again, and then relapsed into her dream of joy and wonder. It would be difficult to say which of the two emotions was the greater,—her joy that her prayer for love should be answered, and so answered,—her wonder that Kavanagh should have selected her! In the tumult of her sensations, and hardly conscious of what she was doing, she folded the note and replaced it in its envelope. Then, for the first time, her eye fell on the superscription. It was "Cecilia Vaughan." Alice fainted.

On recovering her senses, her first act was one of heroism. She sealed the note, attached it to the neck of the pigeon, and sent the messenger rejoicing on his journey. Then her feelings had way, and she wept long and bitterly. Then, with a desperate calmness, she reproved her own weakness and selfishness, and felt that she ought to rejoice in the happiness of her friend, and sacrifice her affection, even her life, to her. Her heart exculpated Kavanagh from all blame. He had not deluded her; she had deluded herself. She alone was in fault; and in deep humiliation, with wounded pride and wounded love, and utter self-abasement, she bowed her head and prayed for consolation and fortitude.

One consolation she already had. The secret was her own. She had not revealed it even to Cecilia. Kavanagh did not suspect it. Public curiosity, public pity, she would not have to undergo.

She was resigned. She made the heroic sacrifice of self, leaving her sorrow to the great physician, Time,—the nurse of care, the healer of all smarts, the soother and consoler of all sorrows. And, thenceforward, she became unto Kavanagh what the moon is to the sun, forever following, forever separated, forever sad!

As a traveler, about to start upon his journey, resolved and yet irresolute, watches the clouds, and notes the struggle between the sunshine and the showers, and says, "It will be fair; I will go,"—and again says, "Ah, no, not yet; the rain is not yet over,"—so at this same hour sat Cecilia Vaughan, resolved and yet irresolute, longing to depart upon the fair journey before her, and yet lingering on the paternal threshold, as if she wished both to stay and to go, seeing the sky was not without its clouds, nor the road without its dangers.

It was a beautiful picture, as she sat there with sweet perplexity in her face, and above it an immortal radiance streaming from her brow. She was like Guercino's Sibyl, with the scroll of fate and the uplifted pen; and the scroll she held contained but three words,—three words that controlled the destiny of a man, and, by their soft impulsion, directed for evermore the current of his thoughts. They were,—

"Come to me!"

The magic syllables brought Kavanagh to her side. The full soul is silent. Only the rising and falling tides rush murmuring through their channels. So sat the lovers, hand in hand; but for a long time neither spake,—neither had need of speech!

XXVII

In the afternoon, Cecilia went to communicate the news to Alice with her own lips, thinking it too important to be entrusted to the wings of the carrier pigeon. As she entered the door, the cheerful doctor was coming out; but this was no unusual apparition, and excited no alarm. Mrs. Archer, too, according to custom, was sitting in the little parlor with her decrepit old neighbor, who seemed almost to have taken up her abode under that roof, so many hours of every day did she pass there.

With a light, elastic step, Cecilia bounded up to Alice's room. She found her reclining in her large chair, flushed and excited. Sitting down by her side, and taking both her hands, she said, with great emotion in the tones of her voice,—

"Dearest Alice, I have brought you some news that I am sure will make you well. For my sake, you will be no longer ill when you hear it. I am engaged to Mr. Kavanagh!"

Alice feigned no surprise at this announcement. She returned the warm pressure of Cecilia's hand, and, looking affectionately in her face, said very calmly,—

"I knew it would be so. I knew that he loved you, and that you would love him."

"How could I help it?" said Cecilia, her eyes beaming with dewy light; "could any one help loving him?"

"No," answered Alice, throwing her arms around Cecilia's neck, and laying her head upon her shoulder; "at least, no one whom he loved. But when did this happen? Tell me all about it, dearest!"

Cecilia was surprised, and perhaps a little hurt, at the quiet, almost impassive manner in which her friend received this great intelligence. She had expected exclamations of wonder and delight, and such a glow of excitement as that with which she was sure she should have hailed the announcement of Alice's engagement. But this momentary annoyance was soon swept away by the tide of her own joyous sensations, as she proceeded to recall to the recollection of her friend the thousand little circumstances that had marked the progress of her love and Kavanagh's; things which she must have noticed, which she could not have forgotten; with questions interspersed at intervals, such as, "Do you recollect when?" and "I am sure you have not forgotten, have you?" and dreamy little pauses of silence, and intercalated sighs. She related to her, also, the perilous adventure of the carrier pigeon; how it had been pursued by the cruel kingfisher; how it had taken refuge in Kavanagh's tower, and had been the bearer of his letter, as well as her own. When she had finished, she felt her bosom wet with the tears of Alice, who was suffering martyrdom on that soft breast, so full of happiness. Tears of bitterness,—tears of blood! And Cecilia, in the exultant temper of her soul at the moment, thought them tears of joy, and pressed Alice closer to her heart, and kissed and caressed her.

"Ah, how very happy you are, Cecilia!" at length sighed the poor sufferer, in that slightly querulous tone, to which Cecilia was not unaccustomed; "how very happy you are, and how very wretched am I! You have all the joy of life, I all its loneliness. How little you will think of me now! How little you will need me! I shall be nothing to you,—you will forget me."

"Never, dearest!" exclaimed Cecilia, with much warmth and sincerity. "I shall love you only the more. We shall both love you. You will now have two friends instead of one."

"Yes; but both will not be equal to the one I lose. No, Cecilia; let us not make to ourselves any illusions. I do not. You cannot now be with me so much and so often as you have been. Even if you were, your thoughts would be elsewhere. Ah, I have lost my friend, when most I needed her!"

Cecilia protested ardently and earnestly, and dilated with eagerness on her little plan of life, in which their romantic friendship was to gain only new strength and beauty from the more romantic love. She was interrupted by a knock at the street door; on hearing which, she paused a moment, and then said,—

"It is Arthur. He was to call for me."

Ah, what glimpses of home, and fireside, and a whole life of happiness for Cecilia, were revealed by that one word of love and intimacy, "Arthur!" and for Alice, what a sentence of doom! what sorrow without a name! what an endless struggle of love and friendship, of duty and inclination! A little quiver of the eyelids and the hands, a hasty motion to raise her head from Cecilia's shoulder,—these were the only outward signs of emotion. But a terrible pang went to her heart; her blood rushed eddying to her brain; and when Cecilia had taken leave of her with the triumphant look of love beaming upon her brow, and an elevation in her whole attitude and bearing, as if borne up by attendant angels, she sank back into her chair, exhausted, fainting, fearing, longing, hoping to die.

And below sat the two old women, talking of moths, and cheap furniture, and what was the best remedy for rheumatism; and from the door went forth two happy hearts, beating side by side with the pulse of youth and hope and joy, and within them and around them was a new heaven and a new earth!

Only those who have lived in a small town can really know how great an event therein is a new engagement. From tongue to tongue passes the swift countersign; from eye to eye flashes the illumination of joy, or the balefire of alarm; the streets and houses ring with it, as with the penetrating, all-pervading sound of the village bell; the whole community feels a thrill of sympathy, and seems to congratulate itself that all the great events are by no means confined to the great towns. As Cecilia and Kavanagh passed arm in arm through the village, many curious eyes watched them from the windows, many hearts grown cold or careless rekindled their household fires of love from the golden altar of God, borne through the streets by those pure and holy hands!

The intelligence of the engagement, however, was received very differently by different persons. Mrs. Wilmerdings wondered, for her part, why anybody wanted to get married at all. The little taxidermist said he knew it would be so from the very first day they had met at his aviary. Miss Hawkins lost suddenly much of her piety and all her patience, and laughed rather hysterically. Mr. Hawkins said it was impossible, but went in secret to consult a friend, an old bachelor, on the best remedy for love; and the old bachelor, as one well versed in such affairs, gravely advised him to think of the lady as a beautiful statue!

Once more the indefatigable schoolgirl took up her pen, and wrote to her foreign correspondent a letter that might rival the famous epistle of Madame de Sévigné to her daughter, announcing the engagement of Mademoiselle Montpensier.

Through the whole of the first page, she told her to guess who the lady was; through the whole of the second, who the gentleman was; the third was devoted to what was said about it in the village; and on the fourth there were two postscripts, one at the top and the other at the bottom, the first stating that they were to be married in the spring, and to go to Italy immediately afterwards, and the last, that Alice Archer was dangerously ill with a fever.

As for the Churchills, they could find no words powerful enough to express their delight, but gave vent to it in a banquet on Thanksgiving Day, in which the wife had all the trouble and the husband all the pleasure. In order that the entertainment might be worthy of the occasion, Mr. Churchill wrote to the city for the best cookery book; and the bookseller, executing the order in all its amplitude, sent him the Practical Guide to the Culinary Art in all its Branches, by Frascatelli, pupil of the celebrated Carême, and Chief Cook to Her Majesty the Queen,— a ponderous volume, illustrated with numerous engravings, and furnished with bills of fare for every month in the year, and any number of persons. This great work was duly studied, evening after evening; and Mr. Churchill confessed to his wife, that, although at first startled by the size of the book, he had really enjoyed it very highly, and had been much pleased to be present in imagination at so many grand entertainments, and to sit opposite the Queen without having to change his dress or the general style of his conversation.

The dinner hour, as well as the dinner itself, was duly debated. Mr. Churchill was in favor of the usual hour of one; but his wife thought it should be an hour later. Whereupon he remarked,—

"King Henry the Eighth dined at ten o'clock and supped at four. His queen's maids of honor had a gallon of ale and a chine of beef for their breakfast."

To which his wife answered,—

"I hope we shall have something a little more refined than that."

The day on which the banquet should take place was next discussed, and both agreed that no day could be so appropriate as Thanksgiving Day; for, as Mrs. Churchill very truly remarked, it was really a day of thanksgiving to Kavanagh. She then said,—

"How very solemnly he read the Governor's Proclamation yesterday! particularly the words 'God save the Commonwealth of Massachusetts!' And what a Proclamation it was! When he spread it out on the pulpit, it looked like a tablecloth!"

Mr. Churchill then asked,—

"What day of the week is the first of December? Let me see,—

'At Dover dwells George Brown, Esquire,
Good Christopher Finch and Daniel Friar!'

Thursday."

"I could have told you that," said his wife, "by a shorter process than your old rhyme. Thanksgiving Day always comes on Thursday."

These preliminaries being duly settled, the dinner was given.

There being only six guests, and the dinner being modelled upon one for twenty-four persons, Russian style in November, it was very abundant. It began with a Colbert soup, and ended with a Nesselrode pudding; but as no allusion was made in the course of the repast to the French names of the dishes, and the mutton, and turnips, and pancakes were all called by their English patronymics, the dinner appeared less magnificent in reality than in the bill of fare, and the guests did not fully appreciate how superb a banquet they were enjoying. The hilarity of the occasion was not marred by any untoward accident; though once or twice Mr. Churchill was much annoyed, and the company much amused, by Master Alfred, who was allowed to be present at the festivities, and audibly proclaimed what was coming, long before it made its appearance. When the dinner was over, several of the guests remembered brilliant and appropriate things they might have said, and wondered they were so dull as not to think of them in season; and when they were all gone, Mr. Churchill remarked to his wife that he had enjoyed himself very much, and that he should like to ask his friends to just such a dinner every week!

XXVIII

THE first snow came. How beautiful it was, falling so silently, all day long, all night long, on the mountains, on the meadows, on the roofs of the living, on the graves of the dead! All white save the river, that marked its course by a winding black line across the landscape; and the leafless trees, that against the leaden sky now revealed more fully the wonderful beauty and intricacy of their branches!

What silence, too, came with the snow, and what seclusion! Every sound was muffled, every noise changed to something soft and musical. No more trampling hoofs,—no more rattling wheels! Only the chiming sleigh bells, beating as swift and merrily as the hearts of children.

All day long, all night long, the snow fell on the village and on the churchyard; on the happy home of Cecilia Vaughan, on the lonely grave of Alice Archer! Yes; for before the winter came she had gone to that land where winter never comes. Her long domestic tragedy was ended. She was dead; and with her had died her secret sorrow and her secret love. Kavanagh never knew what wealth of affection for him faded from the world when she departed; Cecilia never knew what fidelity of friendship, what delicate regard, what gentle magnanimity, what angelic patience had gone with her into the grave; Mr. Churchill never knew, that, while he was exploring the past for records of obscure and unknown martyrs, in his own village, near his own door, before his own eyes, one of that silent sisterhood had passed away into oblivion, unnoticed and unknown.

How often, ah, how often, between the desire of the heart and its fulfilment, lies only the briefest space of time and distance, and yet the desire remains forever unfulfilled! It is so near that we can touch it with the hand, and yet so far away that the eye cannot perceive it. What Mr. Churchill most desired was before him. The Romance he was longing to find and record had really occurred in his neighborhood, among his own friends. It had been set like a picture into the framework of his life, enclosed within his own experience. But he could not see it as an object apart from himself; and as he was gazing at what was remote and strange and indistinct, the nearer incidents of aspiration, love, and death, escaped him. They were too near to be clothed by the imagination with the golden vapors of romance; for the familiar seems trivial, and only the distant and unknown completely fill and satisfy the mind.

The winter did not pass without its peculiar delights and recreations. The singing of the great wood fires; the blowing of the wind over the chimney tops, as if they were organ pipes; the splendor of the spotless snow; the purple wall built round the horizon at sunset; the sea-suggesting pines, with the moan of the billows in their branches, on which the snows were furled like sails; the northern lights; the stars of steel; the transcendent moonlight, and the lovely shadows of the leafless trees upon the snow;—these things did not pass unnoticed nor unremembered. Every one of them made its record upon the heart of Mr. Churchill.

His twilight walks, his long Saturday afternoon rambles, had again become solitary; for Kavanagh was lost to him for such purposes, and his wife was one of those women who never walk. Sometimes he went down to the banks of the frozen river, and saw the farmers crossing it with their heavy-laden sleds, and the Fairmeadow schooner imbedded in the ice; and thought of Lapland sledges, and the song of Kulnasatz, and the dismantled, ice-locked vessels of the explorers in the Arctic Ocean. Sometimes he went to the neighboring lake, and saw the skaters wheeling round their fire, and speeding away before the wind; and in his imagination arose images of the Norwegian Skate-Runners, bearing the tidings of King Charles's death from Frederickshall to Drontheim, and of the retreating Swedish army, frozen to death in its fireless tents among the mountains. And then he would watch the cutting of the ice with ploughs, and the horses dragging the huge blocks to the storehouses, and contrast them with the Grecian mules, bearing the snows of Mount Parnassus to the markets of Athens, in panniers protected from the sun by boughs of oleander and rhododendron.

The rest of his leisure hours were employed in anything and everything save in writing his Romance. A great deal of time was daily consumed in reading the newspapers, because it was necessary, he said, to keep up with the times; and a great deal more in writing a lyceum lecture, on "What Lady Macbeth Might Have Been, Had Her Energies Been Properly Directed." He also made some little progress in a poetical arithmetic, founded on Bhascara's, but relinquished it, because the school committee thought it was not practical enough, and more than hinted that he had better adhere to the old system. And still the vision of the great Romance moved before his mind, august and glorious, a beautiful mirage of the desert.

XXIX

THE wedding did not take place till spring. And then Kavanagh and his Cecilia departed on their journey to Italy and the East,—a sacred mission, a visit like the Apostle's to the Seven Churches, nay, to all the churches of Christendom; hoping by some means to sow in many devout hearts the desire and prophecy that filled his own,—the union of all sects into one universal church of Christ. They intended to be absent one year only; they were gone three. It seemed to their friends that they never would return. But at length they came,—the long absent, the long looked for, the long desired,—bearing with them that delicious perfume of travel, that genial, sunny atmosphere, and soft, Ausonian air, which returning travelers always bring about them.

It was night when they reached the village, and they could not see what changes had taken place in it during their absence. How it had dilated and magnified itself,—how it had puffed itself up, and bedizened itself with flaunting, ostentatious signs,—how it stood, rotund and rubicund with brick, like a portly man, with his back to the fire and both hands in his pockets, warm, expansive, apoplectic, and entertaining a very favorable opinion of himself,—all this they did not see, for the darkness; but Kavanagh beheld it all, and more, when he went forth on the following morning.

How Cecilia's heart beat as they drove up the avenue to the old house! The piny odors in the night air, the solitary light at her father's window, the familiar bark of the dog Major at the sound of the wheels, awakened feelings at once new and old. A sweet perplexity of thought, a strange familiarity, a no less pleasing strangeness! The lifting of the heavy brass latch, and the jarring of the heavy brass knocker as the door closed, were echoes from her childhood. Mr. Vaughan they found, as usual, among his papers in the study;—the same bland, white-haired man, hardly a day older than when they left him there. To Cecilia the whole long absence in Italy became a dream, and vanished away. Even Kavanagh was for the moment forgotten. She was a daughter, not a wife;—she had not been married, she had not been in Italy!

In the morning, Kavanagh sallied forth to find the Fair-meadow of his memory, but found it not. The railroad had completely transformed it. The simple village had become a very precocious town. New shops, with new names over the doors; new streets, with new forms and faces in them; the whole town seemed to have been taken and occupied by a besieging army of strangers. Nothing was permanent but the workhouse, standing alone in the pasture by the river; and, at the end of the street, the schoolhouse, that other workhouse, where in childhood we pick and untwist the cordage of the brain, that, later in life, we may not be obliged to pull to pieces the more material cordage of old ships.

Kavanagh soon turned in despair from the main street into a little green lane, where there were few houses, and where the barberry still nodded over the old stone wall;—a place he had much loved in the olden time for its silence and seclusion. He seemed to have entered his ancient realm of dreams again, and was walking with his hat drawn a little over his eyes. He had not proceeded far, when he was startled by a woman's voice, quite sharp and loud, crying from the opposite side of the lane. Looking up, he beheld a small cottage, against the wall of which rested a ladder, and on this ladder stood the woman from whom the voice came. Her face was nearly concealed by a spacious gingham sunbonnet, and in her right hand she held extended a large brush, with which she was painting the front of her cottage, when interrupted by the approach of Kavanagh, who, thinking she was calling to him, but not understanding what she said, made haste to cross over to her assistance. At this movement her tone became louder and more peremptory; and he could now understand that her cry was rather a warning than an invitation.

"Go away!" she said, flourishing her brush. "Go away! What are you coming down here for, when I am on the ladder, painting my house? If you don't go right about your business, I will come down and——"

"Why, Miss Manchester!" exclaimed Kavanagh; "how could I know that you would be going up the ladder just as I came down the lane?"

"Well, I declare! if it is not Mr. Kavanagh!"

And she scrambled down the ladder backwards with as much grace as the circumstances permitted. She, too, like the rest of his friends in the village, showed symptoms of growing older. The passing years had drunk a portion of the light from her eyes, and left their traces on her cheeks, as birds that drink at lakes leave their footprints on the margin. But the pleasant smile remained, and reminded him of the bygone days, when she used to open for him the door of the gloomy house under the poplars.

Many things had she to ask, and many to tell; and for full half an hour Kavanagh stood leaning over the paling, while she remained among the hollyhocks, as stately and red as the plants themselves. At parting, she gave him one of the flowers for his wife; and, when he was fairly out of sight, again climbed the perilous ladder, and resumed her fresco painting.

Through all the vicissitudes of these later years, Sally had remained true to her principles and resolution. At Mrs. Archer's death, which occurred soon after Kavanagh's wedding, she had retired to this little cottage, bought and paid for by her own savings. Though often urged by Mr. Vaughan's man, Silas, who breathed his soul out upon the air of summer evenings through a keyed bugle, she resolutely refused to marry. In vain did he send her letters written with his own blood,—going barefooted into the brook to be bitten by leeches, and then using his feet as inkstands: she refused again and again. Was it that in some blue chamber, or some little warm back parlor, of her heart, the portrait of the inconstant dentist was still hanging? Alas, no! But as to some hearts it is given in youth to blossom with the fragrant blooms of young desire, so others are doomed by a mysterious destiny to be checked in spring by chill winds, blowing over the bleak common of the world. So had it been with her desires and thoughts of love. Fear now predominated over hope; and to die unmarried had become to her a fatality which she dared not resist.

In the course of his long conversation with Miss Manchester, Kavanagh learned many things about the inhabitants of the town. Mrs. Wilmerdings was still carrying on her labors in the "Dunstable and eleven-braid, open-work and colored straws." Her husband had taken to the tavern, and often came home very late, "with a brick in his hat," as Sally expressed it. Their son and heir was far away in the Pacific, on board a whaleship. Miss Amelia Hawkins remained unmarried, though possessing a talent for matrimony which amounted almost to genius. Her brother, the poet, was no more. Finding it impossible to follow the old bachelor's advice, and look upon Miss Vaughan as a beautiful statue, he made one or two attempts, but in vain, to throw himself away on unworthy objects, and then died. At this event, two elderly maidens went into mourning simultaneously, each thinking herself engaged to him; and suddenly went out of it again, mutually indignant with each other, and mortified with themselves. The little taxidermist was still hopping about in his aviary, looking more than ever like his gray African parrot. Mrs. Archer's house was uninhabited.

XXX

KAVANAGH continued his walk in the direction of Mr. Churchill's residence. This, at least, was unchanged,—quite unchanged. The same white front; the same brass knocker; the same old wooden gate, with its chain and ball; the same damask roses under the windows; the same sunshine without and within. The outer door and study door were both open, as usual in the warm weather; and at the table sat Mr. Churchill, writing. Over each ear was a black and inky stump of a pen, which, like the two ravens perched on Odin's shoulders, seemed to whisper to him all that passed in heaven and on earth. On this occasion, their revelations were of the earth. He was correcting school exercises.

The joyful welcome of Mr. Churchill, as Kavanagh entered, and the cheerful sound of their voices, soon brought Mrs. Churchill to the study,—her eyes bluer than ever, her cheeks fairer, her form more round and full. The children came in also,— Alfred grown to boy's estate and exalted into a jacket; and the baby that was, less than two years behind him, and catching all his falling mantles, and all his tricks and maladies.

Kavanagh found Mr. Churchill precisely where he left him. He had not advanced one step,—not one. The same dreams, the same longings, the same aspirations, the same indecision. A thousand things had been planned, and none completed. His imagination seemed still to exhaust itself in running, before it tried to leap the ditch. While he mused, the fire burned in other brains. Other hands wrote the books he dreamed about. He freely used his good ideas in conversation, and in letters; and they were straightway wrought into the texture of other men's books, and so lost to him forever. His work on Obscure

Martyrs was anticipated by Mr. Hathaway, who, catching the idea from him, wrote and published a series of papers on Unknown Saints, before Mr. Churchill had fairly arranged his materials. Before he had written a chapter of his great Romance, another friend and novelist had published one on the same subject.

Poor Mr. Churchill! So far as fame and external success were concerned, his life certainly was a failure. He was, perhaps, too deeply freighted, too much laden by the head, to ride the waves gracefully. Every sea broke over him,—he was half the time under water!

All his defects and mortifications he attributed to the outward circumstances of his life, the exigencies of his profession, the accidents of chance. But, in reality, they lay much deeper than this. They were within himself. He wanted the all-controlling, all-subduing will. He wanted the fixed purpose that sways and bends all circumstances to its uses, as the wind bends the reeds and rushes beneath it.

In a few minutes, and in that broad style of handling, in which nothing is distinctly defined, but everything clearly suggested, Kavanagh sketched to his friends his three years' life in Italy and the East. And then, turning to Mr. Churchill, he said,—

"And you, my friend,—what have you been doing all this while? You have written to me so rarely that I have hardly kept pace with you. But I have thought of you constantly. In all the old cathedrals; in all the lovely landscapes; among the Alps and Apennines; in looking down on Duomo d'Ossola; at the Inn of Baveno; at Gaeta; at Naples; in old and mouldy Rome; in older Egypt; in the Holy Land; in all galleries and churches and ruins; in our rural retirement at Fiesoli;—whenever I have seen anything beautiful, I have thought of you, and of how much you would have enjoyed it!"

Mr. Churchill sighed; and then, as if, with a touch as masterly, he would draw a picture that should define nothing, but suggest everything, he said,—

"You have no children, Kavanagh; we have five."

"Ah, so many already!" exclaimed Kavanagh. "A living Pentateuch! A beautiful Pentapylon, or five-gated temple of Life! A charming number!"

"Yes," answered Mr. Churchill; "a beautiful number; Juno's own; the wedding of the first even and first uneven numbers; the number sacred to marriage, but having no reference, direct or indirect, to the Pythagorean novitiate of five years of silence."

"No; it certainly is not the vocation of children to be silent," said Kavanagh, laughing. "That would be out of nature; saving always the children of the brain, which do not often make so much noise in the world as we desire. I hope a still larger family of these has grown up around you during my absence."

"Quite otherwise," answered the schoolmaster, sadly. "My brain has been almost barren of songs. I have only been trifling; and I am afraid, that, if I play any longer with Apollo, the untoward winds will blow the discus of the god against my forehead, and strike me dead with it, as they did Hyacinth of old."

"And your Romance,—have you been more successful with that? I hope it is finished, or nearly finished?"

"Not yet begun," said Mr. Churchill. "The plan and characters still remain vague and indefinite in my mind. I have not even found a name for it."

"That you can determine after the book is written," suggested Kavanagh. "You can name it, for instance, as the old Heimskringla was named, from the initial word of the first chapter."

"Ah! that was very well in the olden time, and in Iceland, when there were no quarterly reviews. It would be called affectation now."

"I see you still stand a little in awe of opinion. Never fear that. The strength of criticism lies only in the weakness of the thing criticized."

"That is the truth, Kavanagh; and I am more afraid of deserving criticism than of receiving it. I stand in awe of my own opinion. The secret demerits of which we alone, perhaps, are conscious, are often more difficult to bear than those which have been publicly censured in us, and thus in some degree atoned for."

"I will not say," replied Kavanagh, "that humility is the only road to excellence, but I am sure that it is one road."

"Yes, humility; but not humiliation," sighed Mr. Churchill, despondingly. "As for excellence, I can only desire it, and dream of it; I cannot attain to it; it lies too far from me; I cannot reach it. These very books about me here, that once stimulated me to action, have now become my accusers. They are my Eumenides, and drive me to despair."

"My friend," said Kavanagh, after a short pause, during which he had taken note of Mr. Churchill's sadness, "that is not always excellent which lies far away from us. What is remote and difficult of access we are apt to overrate; what is really best for us lies always within our reach, though often overlooked. To speak frankly, I am afraid this is the case with your Romance. You are evidently grasping at something which lies beyond the confines of your own experience, and which, consequently, is only a play of shadows in the realm of fancy. The figures have no vitality; they are only outward shows, wanting inward life. We can give to others only what we have."

"And if we have nothing worth giving?" interrupted Mr. Churchill.

"No man is so poor as that. As well might the mountain streamlets say they have nothing worth giving to the sea, because they are not rivers. Give what you have. To some one, it may be better than you dare to think. If you had looked nearer for the materials of your Romance, and had set about it in earnest, it would now have been finished."

"And burned, perhaps," interposed Mr. Churchill; "or sunk with the books of Simon Magus to the bottom of the Dead Sea."

"At all events, you would have had the pleasure of writing it. I remember one of the old traditions of art, from which you may perhaps draw a moral. When Raphael desired to paint his Holy Family, for a long time he strove in vain to express the idea that filled and possessed his soul. One morning, as he walked beyond the city gates, meditating the sacred theme, he beheld, sitting beneath a vine at her cottage door, a peasant woman, holding a boy in her arms, while another leaned upon her knee, and gazed at the approaching stranger. The painter found here, in real life, what he had so long sought for in vain in the realms of his imagination; and quickly, with his chalk pencil, he sketched, upon the head of a wine cask that stood near them, the lovely group, which afterwards, when brought into full perfection, became the transcendent Madonna della Seggiola."

"All this is true," replied Mr. Churchill, "but it gives me no consolation. I now despair of writing anything excellent. I have no time to devote to meditation and study. My life is given to others, and to this destiny I submit without a murmur; for I have the satisfaction of having labored faithfully in my calling, and of having perhaps trained and incited others to do what I shall never do. Life is still precious to me for its many uses, of which the writing of books is but one. I do not complain, but accept this destiny, and say, with that pleasant author, Marcus Antoninus, 'Whatever is agreeable to thee shall be agreeable to me, O graceful Universe! nothing shall be to me too early or too late, which is seasonable to thee! Whatever thy seasons bear shall be joyful fruit to me, O Nature! from thee are all things; in thee they subsist; to thee they return. Could one say, Thou dearly beloved city of Cecrops? and wilt thou not say, Thou dearly beloved city of God?' "

"Amen!" said Kavanagh. "And, to follow your quotation with another, 'The gale that blows from God we must endure, toiling but not repining.' "

Here Mrs. Churchill, who had something of Martha in her, as well as of Mary, and had left the room when the conversation took a literary turn, came back to announce that dinner was ready, and Kavanagh, though warmly urged to stay, took his leave, having first obtained from the Churchills the promise of a visit to Cecilia during the evening.

"Nothing done! nothing done!" exclaimed he, as he wended his way homeward, musing and meditating. "And shall all these lofty aspirations end in nothing? Shall the arms be thus stretched forth to encircle the universe, and come back empty against a bleeding, aching breast?"

And the words of the poet came into his mind, and he thought them worthy to be written in letters of gold, and placed above every door in every house, as a warning, a suggestion, an incitement:—

> "Stay, stay the present instant!
> Imprint the marks of wisdom on its wings!
> O, let it not elude thy grasp, but like
> The good old patriarch upon record,
> Hold the fleet angel fast until he bless thee!"

DATE	
DEC 1 6 '75	
DEC 1 9 1976	
GAYLORD	